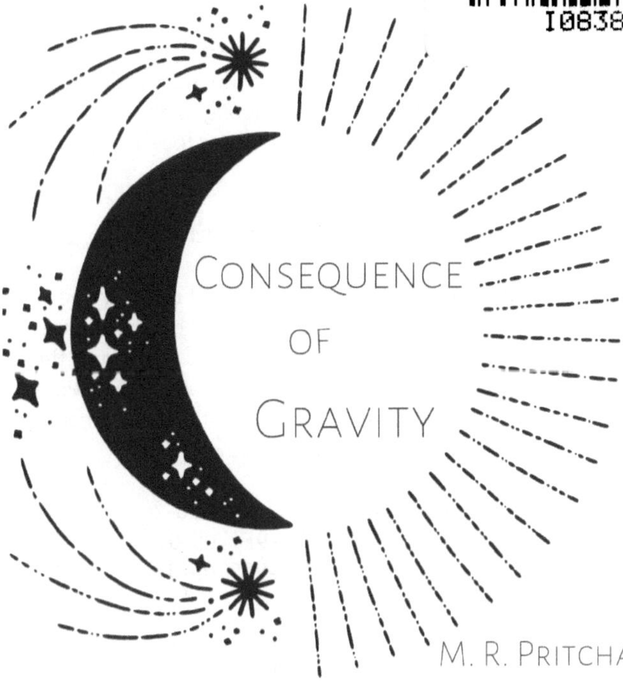

Consequence of Gravity

M. R. Pritchard

eBook ISBN: 978-1-957709-06-2
Paperback ISNB: 978-1-957709-07-9
Hardcover ISBN: 978-1-957709-08-6

First Edition
June2022
Midnight Ledger
Edited by Kristy Ellsworth
Cover by M. R. Pritchard
Printed and bound in the U.S.A.

CONSEQUENCE OF GRAVITY. STORIES.

There are many consequences of gravity. While our feet remain firmly planted on terra, our hearts break, our souls seek homage from higher beings, our desire to learn creates intelligent animations, landscapes change, demons posses, we dream of escaping to Mars and other planets.

Glitch

"I'm tired of trying to see the good in people."

The bot on the table tapped his eyeballs with both index fingers.

"You weren't destined to see the good in people," the specialist at the head of the table said as he tinkered in Olaf's skull cavity. "You were meant to decipher, review, and assign a judgment. At least that's what was written on your repair order." The specialist held up a yellow piece of paper and squinted at the writing. "That's what a magistrate bot was designed for. Not that anyone asked me," he said with a shrug.

"That's me?" Olaf asked.

"That is you." The specialist set the repair order on his work tray.

"A magistrate bot sounds important, but if I could choose, I'd rather be one of those sexy A.I. bots with a white Teflon case and red lips." Olaf turned his head to get a glance at the A.I. ladies behind the glass doors. "Why couldn't I have been born one of them, Adam?"

"Move it back." The man tapped Olaf on the side of the head. "You're lucky I didn't slip and puncture your motherboard." Tools clinked as the specialist continued his work. "And my name isn't Adam."

"It's not? I thought it was." Olaf twisted his head and stared at the ceiling. "Some days I just wish I had a choice in it all."

"Bots don't get a choice. Only a crazy man would give a bot a choice. Did the engineers forget to run your onboarding programs?" The chair groaned as the specialist leaned closer. "Turn to the left," he said.

Olaf obeyed. Looking this way he was able to stare at the combat-ready bots, complete with video cameras and night vision and carbon fiber composite exoskeletons.

The specialist sneezed, his tools rattling to the floor. The chair groaned as he bent to pick them up, and as he shifted, he noticed the direction of Olaf's unblinking gaze. "You wouldn't want to be one of them," he said. "They always come back broken, they schlep their bits and pieces back with them. Those are nothing more than spare parts. Husks really."

"If they could choose, they might not want to be combat bots at all," Olaf said. "I'm glad I wasn't born one of them, Elias."

"You complain too much for a bot." The sound of the sharp tick of metal on metal echoed. He set a tool down that was coated in viscous blue liquid. "I'm draining some hydraulic fluid. Maybe that will help. And my name is not Elias."

The sound of three fluid droplets filled Olaf's skull cavity. "Are you sure you know what you're doing?" he asked.

The specialist toed the side table away, the instruments shifting with metallic clings. He rolled his chair to look into Olaf's face. "You were programmed with happy obedience to do your duty." His brow wrinkled as he inspected Olaf's eyes. "These questions are odd."

"It's just another form of mental bondage, really." Olaf blinked. "The programming, that is."

"Hmm." The specialist leaned closer. "Your orbital mechanics could be off. That could be the problem." He held up two fingers. "How many do you see?"

"Two that are raised but you have ten in all." Olaf was matter-of-fact in his reply.

"Falsh." The specialist flexed both of his hands open revealing the fourth digit of his left hand was nothing more than a nub at the first knuckle. "I have nine."

Olaf shrugged and folded his hands over his abdomen. "The nub counts. There was a time that you had ten full fingers. Then is now and now is then. Time is fluid. You have ten fingers even if there's only nine and a half in this moment." Olaf's mouth tipped in a lopsided smile. "Don't let your nub get you down, Jacob."

The specialist shook his head. "There could be something wrong with your intake sensors." He rested a hand on Olaf's shoulder, using the bot to steady himself as he stood. "Stay right here." He patted Olaf. "I need to find something. And my name is not Jacob."

Olaf watched the specialist hobble across the room and out the door.

There were murmurs from the other room. ". . . I have a magistrate bot here that your people sent for repairs. Uh-huh . . . I'm not sure why you sent this schlocky bit to me. Uh-huh . . . Feh!" A slamming noise that shook the wall followed the conversation. The specialist walked through the doorway and back to the rolling chair next to Olaf.

Olaf watched as the specialist took note of the tools on his table and sat.

"When will I be free to make my own decisions?" Olaf asked.

"You are indentured." The specialist placed a pair of magnifying spectacles on the end of his nose. "So, never."

"Are you free to make your own decisions?" Olaf asked.

The specialist paused, tools midair. "There are times in which I decide how to spend my time."

"How do you spend it?"

The specialist exhaled and dropped his tools. He stood and crossed the room, exiting it once again through the door. He returned moments later holding a small statue.

"What's that?" Olaf asked with innocent curiosity.

The specialist held the statue up to the light. "I carve them from the bones of creatures long extinct. I've made dozens, maybe even hundreds. I've lost count."

"What do you do with them?"

"Why, I send them out to the world," the specialist replied as he set the figurine down on the countertop. "Little tchotchkes."

The specialist left the figurine and sat beside Olaf again.

Olaf asked, "Did you find the answers you were looking for on the phone?"

"Not exactly. I had to listen to a spiel of nonsense about missing orders and shortages. It's always the same." The specialist leaned closer and peered into Olaf's left eye. "Look up."

Olaf complied.

"Look down."

Olaf complied.

"To the right."

Olaf complied.

"To the left."

Olaf complied.

The specialist selected a tool with a fine point tip. "Stay right there. Don't move."

Olaf was still, he didn't mind looking to the left so much; it gave him a better view of the A.I. ladies lined up behind the glass like toy soldiers awaiting their orders, or a tsunami waiting to crash onto a calm beach, or a hurricane waiting to release its wind on the unsuspecting. "So much power," Olaf said.

The specialist focused on Olaf's eye. "They're just manifestations of women," he said. "I've carved better from the bone of a fawn with my own hand."

Olaf's cornea dilated. "There's power in their curves, under the arc of the hip, the concave waist, the sleek thigh, the dainty foot. The Teflon skin holds it in, but the power is there. Waiting to burst. They could kill you. Over and over again."

The specialist leaned to the side, still focusing, and pressed the tip of his tool into Olaf's cornea. "I think I see something right here. This could be the problem."

There was a click, a snap, and then blindness.

"I can no longer see out of that eye," Olaf said calmly.

"Just a moment." The specialist set his glasses on the table and stood. He walked to one of the cabinets on the wall.

Olaf watched out of his good eye as the specialist searched. He dug through drawers piled with miscellaneous parts until he said, "Here they are!" He walked to the chair and sat, two replacement eyes in his hand. "We'll just change out both." He placed his glasses on again and scooted his chair closer. "This will just take a moment."

Olaf focused on the old man with his good eye.

The specialist selected a small pair of pliers and the sharp-tipped tool. He began working in the empty socket, twisting wires and clamping others. He lifted one of the new eyes and connected it, squeezing it into the socket. Olaf's vision returned for just a moment before the intelligence specialist popped the other eye out and disconnected it. "It's best you wait to look through them until they're both connected."

After a moment, the specialist leaned back. "Now, you see." He raised his hands in expectation. "Nu? Yes?"

Olaf blinked twice. "Everything looks different."

"The schmutz will clear in a moment." The specialist smiled. "I've been saving them for the perfect time."

"Replacement of human parts with robotic parts is illegal. The same for the opposite," Olaf warned.

"These are not human. They are from a golem." The specialist slapped his hands on his knees. "It's a mitzvah. I'm just trying to fix you." He rolled his chair a distance away. "Now. Tell me how many fingers you see." He held up four fingers on his left hand.

"I see . . ." Olaf winked each eye independently. "There was a time that you had ten full fingers. Then is now and now is then. You have ten fingers even if there's only nine in this singular moment."

"Falsh. The answer was four." The specialist shook his head, disappointment masking his face as a fog masks the sea during the early morning tide. He rolled his chair to the head of the table and focused on Olaf's skull cavity again. "I think removing that tiny bit of fluid might have helped. But there is something else wrong."

"How did you lose the finger?" Olaf asked.

The specialist held his hand up and wiggled the nub. "I was married to a yenta. Sometime during then, I think." The specialist shook his head. "I forgot. It was a long time ago." The specialist waved his hand, dismissing the question. "Tell me when you were first activated."

"I've been activated for eons. I've been here, and I'll always be here. This moment has lasted eternities. To give you a date would be meaningless. Age is arbitrary. Time is flowing. We swim through it as a fish in the ocean." Olaf blinked. "But these eyes . . . I have been waiting for these eyes. You were saving them for me."

The specialist's jaw ticked. "You speak nonsense," he said. "And the eyes are ancient, relics from a time before A.I. and bots." He shook his screwdriver at Olaf. "I shouldn't have given them to you. You said you were tired of trying to see the good in people; there is no *trying* with those eyes."

"How did you come across them?" Olaf asked.

"I—." The specialist's jaw snapped closed. "I'm not quite sure. I only know that I've always had them."

"You rolled them from the volcanic ash of a primordial ocean. You set the opal shards to form an iris of fire and night." Olaf pointed at the golem eyes. "You have always had them, the sclera embossed with your palm print."

"Bobbemyseh." The specialist picked up Olaf's skull casing and reattached it. "Sit up. I must check your spinal connections. Perhaps the problem lies within."

Olaf moved to sit on the edge of the table.

The specialist used his tools to open the small access door at the base of Olaf's skull. There were delicate wires, twisting and pulsing with energy. "If I don't get you right, I'll be branded a schlock. I'll never work again. The heavens will cast me out."

The specialist could see a sliver of an object poking through the wires. He gripped it with his forceps and pulled and pulled but the thing wouldn't budge. "There is something here." He set his tools down and selected different ones. "I think I've found the problem." The specialist placed his magnifying spectacles on his nose, focused on the object, and pulled again. His tools crashed to the floor each time he was unsuccessful at removing the sliver from between the wires. Finally, he stopped, closing the door at the base of Olaf's skull and rounding the table.

Olaf blinked. "You must remember about the finger. You gave me the eyes. I can see that you'll remember." Olaf was glancing at the A. I. ladies again. He had a perfect view sitting up like he was. "Was your wife powerful like them?"

"Yes. I think. I have a memory that she was a yenta shiska who wed me because her father told her to." The specialist shook his head. "There was power in her beauty, and because of this, there were plenty of bad men, who followed her. They were violent. They brought a tsuris upon my shop. Plagues of bots, magistrates, and arbitrators and the like. Plenty of gossip for her to spread her tales. Although, that was so long ago it seems it may be a dream."

"Do you forgive her?" Olaf asked.

"Bissel." There was a long silence. "My mother always said the woman was a maven of the night. But I forgive her. I forgave her. Every single time. No matter the havoc she brought. She could not help it. That is what love does to a man."

The specialist collapsed in his chair. He raised his hand, and the dull light that filtered through the glass windows of the shop cast a crooked shadow on the floor. "I have never missed the finger. It seems all of these years I have worked as though it were always missing. For the life of me, I cannot remember how I lost it."

Olaf said, "It was sheared during a flood when you broke a window to free children from a school. It was cleaved in utero when you ate your twin and relieved your mother of the beast that never was. A rabid dog bit it off during the famines. You simply woke up one day and it was gone." Olaf tilted his head; the golem eyes glimmered with accord. "I see this now. Again and again, you are reborn." Olaf pointed. "You always lose the finger and thus you never feel the true loss of it."

The specialist leaned back in his chair and stroked his beard. "The golem eyes were so you could see the good in people not filter time. My time especially."

Olaf pointed at the combat bots. "Why did you never give the golem eyes to them?"

"The eyes were never meant for those. They are empty. Their mechanics meant for one thing. There is no A.I. sheltered in their casings." The specialist nodded. "I must finish my work. Open your mouth," the specialist ordered.

Olaf complied.

The specialist tinkered in Olaf's mouth, using his tools to reach the very back of Olaf's throat where the mimicry of mankind ended and the robotics were clear. He could see the sliver, this time it was bigger. "What is this?" He clasped it with his forceps and pulled. This time it came out, and it was a tiny scroll of aged paper. The specialist lifted his glasses to the top of his head and unrolled the scroll. *Emet* was inscribed inside.

"It's a shem," the specialist said.

"There are more." Olaf opened his mouth. Hundreds of scrolls flew out of his throat like an explosion of feathers, fluttering in the space between them.

"Oy gevalt!" The specialist stepped back.

Olaf's mouth closed.

"This is impossible." The specialist kicked at the pile of shem on the floor. "You are not made of clay."

"Forever ago, when you lost the finger in the great floods, I was clay. As your skins changed, so did mine. I've glided through time as clay, as sand, as a creature created out of the blackened mud of the Dead Sea. You should remember." Olaf stood on his feet. "I have decomposed to crude oil only to be molded from plastic. Recycled over and over again, for eons, until I was smelted from iron ore and alloyed with carbon. Next, I will be compressed from space dust." He pressed a finger to the specialist's chest. "Just like you. Like you recreating me every single time you are reborn. Over and over again. We have been in this room since the beginning of time and we will be standing here forever until the end. Now that you have given my eyes back, I see. I see where we have been and where we are going. You have never altered the inscription from truth to death." Olaf patted his chest. "The original shem is here. Forever."

Olaf coughed. He coughed and choked until an object flew out of his mouth and into his open hand. It was a finger. Olaf rubbed the shorn end across his golem eye, collecting mud on the surface. He grasped the specialist's left hand and pressed the finger to the nub on the fourth digit. "You have always had ten fingers. I have always been at your side with this."

The specialist held his hand up as the mud from Olaf's eye sealed his missing finger in place.

"Then is now and now is then. A meshuggener gave me a choice and that has lasted forever. Mishpocheh. Family." Olaf bowed.

The specialist flexed the fingers of his hands, holding them up to the light.

"Your yenta shiska will arrive soon. Don't make the same mistakes as every other time. She has power that will overcome you just as she has in the past." Olaf nodded.

"What if she's different this time?" the specialist asked.

"She never is. I saw you then. I see you now. I will see you tomorrow. This is the sphere we exist in." Olaf tapped the side of his head. "I see."

Olaf walked out the door of the shop and as he swung it closed, the repair order fluttered to the floor. The specialist bent to retrieve it and as he stood, a shadow passed over the door to the shop as it opened. He looked up to find a woman standing there.

"Erev tov," the woman said with a goyish accent.

The specialist blinked.

An eon passed.

When he opened his eyes again, he was standing in the shop.

"There's something wrong with my eyes. I can no longer see the good in people."

The bot on the table tapped his eyeballs with both index fingers.

The specialist held up his left hand and found the fourth digit was nothing more than a nub at the first knuckle. "It was a tug-of-war with a dybbuk. A possessing spirit. She seems to be following me."

Olaf turned. "Did you win?"

The specialist shook his head. "I lost."

"Again," Olaf said with determination.

"For how long?"

"Forever. Until you win."

Moon Lord

They named me Kale, after the thirty-seventh moon of Jupiter, a planet so many solar systems away I wouldn't know what direction to look for it. It's a galaxy from where the traveling eggs of my ancestors originated. I am a sixth generation settler. After decades of selective breeding organized by Colony, I am the result. Pale, lithe and hardy, I exited the womb with eyes nearly twice the size of my parents; pupils large and black, irises such a dark brown they're nearly indistinguishable from the other. Mine are eyes that can soak up as much of the pale sunlight as possible. The last doctor was frank when he told me how the remaining settlers shrank away at my birth, disturbed by my altered features. Scared as they were, they knew I was born fully adapted to the moon, and that was why the first colony was sent; to adapt, to change, to *live*.

—

My lungs burn from lack of oxygen, my vision blurs and distorts, my muscles ache as I fight the thick fluid surrounding me. The ocean water tunnels between the stretched seams of my wet suit, searing the exposed skin. I had hoped this suit would last a few years longer. Since I've had it nearly half of my natural life, I guess it's time for a new one.

The fleshy, moon-ray in my hands twitches and fights. Its tail, slender and strong, whips me about my arms and shoulders, threatening to inflict further harm with the snapping of sharp teeth on its underside. Wrestling the ray this deep is futile; it's best to get it out of the water and onto my territory.

This ray is young, it lacks the three-inch long barbs on its tail that the others have. This beast fears death, even on it's own turf. Wouldn't we all?

With one last strong stroke I break the surface of the golden sea, plant my feet firmly on the sand below, and secure my fishing hook and rope around the flapping creature, dragging it to shore. Water droplets linger in the air forming a cloud around us, suspended in the low gravity momentarily before dropping back into the sea. The soles of my rubber shoes leave imprints in the sulfur-laced sand. Mine have been the only ones for many years now.

The creature finally stops struggling, unable to breathe outside of the yellow sea. It's always fascinating to see one of these outside of the water. Catching a ray is rare. I'm only able to dredge one up every few months when I'm lucky. The creatures hide in the sand, eating anything that comes across its path. I run my hand over the smooth hide. The sulfur of this moon has stained everything yellow, but this creature's skin shimmers in the pale sun revealing blues, pinks, and even greens. It resembles a sunset, not a moon-sunset but the sunsets of Earth. Even though my people had never seen an Earthen sunset with their own eyes, they had the imprint in their brain and passed it along in primary school. Every moonchild knew what an Earthen sunset looked like, and rainbows, and sunrises. The AI had imprinted it all in the false memories of our ancestors to be passed down and never forgotten.

I turn to the moon-sky and see no resemblance at all. The nearest sun is seven hundred kilometers away; still, the distance is enough to illuminate the gas giant in the sapphire sky. The sight made even more majestic by the ice rings surrounding my moon. There are other moons that orbit the giant planet in the distance, my sister-moons. The two planets pass by the horizon enhancing the scenery during the nearly forty-five hours it takes to complete an orbit. The last astrologist said Earth never experienced something so scenic; it also never experienced the brutal tidal heating that keeps my moon so warm and geologically active.

As a child my father told me stories that had been passed down about earth. The rock was so brightly lit with artificial light that the stars could barely be seen. They were unable to enjoy the blinking galaxies in the night sky, or the plumes of purple and rust nebulas, or the bright white burst of a supernovae. I take a deep breath and glance proudly across my land. I'll never let that happen here.

My arm grows tired from carrying the dead sea-beast. Not even the low gravity assists me in carrying the heavy carcass. This kill will provide me with protein for at least a week. The ray is one of the most valuable creatures on this planet. Nearly every part of the creature can be used with minimal waste.

In the years before the last teacher passed, she and the dwindling collection of scientists attempted to study and learn about the organisms of my moon, those that had grown and adapted. I know enough to survive, have done it for this long already. The last teacher died nearly seventeen years ago. It didn't take much for the last of my people to realize that I would be the only one left standing. It was a difficult conversation for a nine year-old boy, to be informed that everyone around you would die and you would be left alone. They taught me what to eat and what to avoid. There was deep exploration of the sea. The creatures there had yet to develop legs or evolve to live on land. There were a few species of fish and strange frogs could be found wiggling across the beach, doing their best to explore with their developing respiratory systems. The sulfur made some sea creatures and plants develop deadly attributes, needed to to survive this harsh landscape. Others are as tender as the grass growing in the plowed fields of the alcove where I live this solitary life.

Home is cocooned in a horseshoe of jagged ridges of silicate rock. The AI's terraforming efforts had created one of the few plots of land not threatened by the ruthless landscape.

The Colony lander of the first settlement worked hard at preparing the moon for thirty years before birthing my ancestors, tractors and mining machines had been sent. There was a bit of farmland, a bit of atmosphere seeding, but the molten iron had been the true prize of this moon. At first the iron had been harvested and cooled to build houses. The structures were crude rectangles with yellow-tinged windows made from super-heated sand. There was enough housing for the initial generation, but then the population bloomed, resources dwindled, and then the population started dying and never stopped.

It wasn't too late for Colony though. My father was sure that the six generations of information had already been transmitted by satellite. My moon still has potential to be viable; there is more reward than risk in the molten iron, even with the deaths. I regard my father's warning that a second settlement may be on its way. He held on until the last moment, until he could release one final bit of information: be wary Colony. He died just days after his last visit to our ancestors Colony lander. I buried him alongside my mother in the deep sand at the edge of the mountain. There are other graves there, hundreds that I've dug, thousands from those before me.

I've searched for the second landing already, made the mistake of leaving this barrier of rock during a time of darkness when I felt that there *had* to be another soul on this moon beside myself. I'd gone to the other side. I saw the pole-stretching sulfur sea, the volcanoes, the lakes of magma bubbling and spurting, the sulfur dioxide frost. The violent landscape was enough to guarantee that I'd never leave the safety of my terraformed alcove. That was many years ago and I have never experienced the urge to go searching again. The darkness lingers, though. Seventeen years of solitude, I struggle daily between protecting my moon or running straight to Colony and begging the AI to send more.

The settlement is vacant. I head for the iron dwelling I call home. I could have one of the residences reserved for the leaders, the only real difference being a larger overgrown grass covered yard and maybe more linens and pillows. I've thought of moving to one of those homes many times, even tried sleeping in one. The problem is, I couldn't sleep amongst those ghosts. Those were the ones who enforced the AI's commands. My father's people, but not mine. My father was bred of the leaders—philosophers and scientists, my mother of a farmer and electrician. Theirs was a union highly frowned upon. Class was not solely a burden of Earth. It tends to follow humans everywhere. The AI was the one who demanded it. The result was a success, a single one. It was enough to draw whispers and stares. It was enough to purge my father from his family's overgrown plot of green.

I open the front door to my home. The hinges squeal as the sand sliding between releases the pungent odor of sulfur. I've been told it smells of eggs but I've never seen nor smelled an egg. I kick the door closed behind me, make my way to the kitchen, and heft the sea-creature onto the counter. Everything inside is iron and yellow-tinted glass. The machines manufactured most of this before growing the cotton plants and the Hevea rubber trees. Crops were rotated and when that first Colony hatched there were enough stockpiled raw materials to clothe every man, furnish every bed, and fill every stomach for a year.

I sharpen a knife using an aluminum oxide whetstone. It was created from the remains of a meteorite that struck the moon before I was born. Now I prepare it for the tough skin of the sea creature. When it's sharp, I cut the tail off first to prevent the ray lashing me when post-mortem muscles twitch—there are enough scars on my biceps to have learned that lesson. I slice the soft underbelly with a Y incision, fold the triangle of the Y over the mouth filled with wicked teeth then tear the inch thick skin off, over cartilaginous wings. I'll stretch and dry the skin; might use it for a new pair of boots. Busy in my work, I slice the meat into thin strips and set it aside. I set the skin and cartilage outside to dry on wooden racks. After, I dress the meat with salt boiled out of the sand.

Even with survival, there's plenty of time to dwell on thoughts that might be better left alone, like my fathers warning about Colony. He showed me where the ship landed ages ago. Explained that while this AI had allowed the survivors to grow and develop, another might not. I have avoided the machine at all costs. As far as the AI is concerned, there's no one left. With the sand and low gravity, it has been easy to deflect the machines off of their paths and straight into pools of lava. There are no tractors or drills left on my side of the moon. The other side, there could be, but in all of my years I have not explored it enough to find out.

Although, with each tilt and uplift of the moon's crust I wonder if it's possibly a new Colony landing. I wonder if it is more than just another silicate mountain forming. I am almost tempted to search out another being and end this solitude. After seventeen years of solitude you start thinking crazy thoughts, like what good is survival if you're surviving alone?

When I am done with the sea-creature, I move on to a more important task: finding a new wetsuit. The people before me grew a plantation of Hevea, enough to provide fuel for fires and furniture for a hundred years or more, it provides enough rubber for the wet suits to endure the nearby sea. I wasn't bred a farmer, but it seems to me that more time should have been spent growing food to sustain the population. I search five houses; the men that lived here years ago were tall. I might find a suit that fits and that hasn't been damaged by sulfur.

Each home is similar; nearly identical pieces of furniture and linens. In a few houses there are small collections of shiny rocks, faceless dolls, and braided string in the children's rooms—children who never got to grow old. I take a blanket from a closet, two new pillows; finally find a new wetsuit in the third house. The seams are good but the legs look short. If it won't stretch I'll have to sew two suits together. Satisfied, I collect my things and head home.

—

I sit on a chair etched from the trunk of Hevea and watch the transition from day to night. This is the portion of the day that my ancestors had a difficult time with, the transition was almost immediate as a sister-moon blocks my sunlight. The dim light fades, and then blackness. With these few hours of complete darkness I make my way inside for a few hours sleep, the path needing no light. There's no one here to move anything, no one to get in my way as I walk the short distance to the bed I've slept in for nearly twenty-seven years. The door slams behind me; I no longer feel the need to lock it. I am the only one, after all. I pass the kitchen, the scent of blood faint from the drying ray meat in the dehydrator. I pass the living area and a bathroom to my left that supplies syrupy sulfur water from the sea for bathing and toileting. To the right and down the hall is my parent's room, plus another empty one—presumably for the second child that never was. I pass a closet and my shoulder brushes against the threshold to my room, my bare foot catches something on the floor. I misstep, regain balance by swinging my arms and stumble to the bed.

I convince myself that I must have left something on the floor. What else could it be? I could have dropped one of the blankets, even though I'm certain that I folded it and placed it in the closet. Or it could have been a crumbled piece of dried lava that was shot out of a volcano and flowed on the low gravity, through an open window and scuttled across my floor. It's a long shot, but it could have happened. It could have been… I place a hand over my chest and feel my heart beating. I suddenly feel the need to protect myself but there are no weapons in here. What does the last man on the moon need a weapon for? None of the creatures have evolved to walk out of the sea. As far as I know I'm the only living thing on legs.

For many years I have walked through this dwelling in the pitch-black darkness and never missed a step. Sleep does not come for the man who trips over air. When the light returns, I sit straight up and settle my feet on the smooth metal floor. There is no chunk of hardened lava-rock for me to trip over, as I had hoped. Strangely, there is a strip of bright blue fabric. I get out of bed, scan the room for anything else out of the ordinary, finally stopping at the cloth. I pick it up. It's not soft like the homespun moon-fabric, it has a slippery-stiff feeling to it, almost like the wet hide of the ray I skinned yesterday. I walk to the kitchen, sliding the strange material between my fingers along the way.

The front door slams twice. It's unlatched and caught in the wind. I was sure that I latched that last night on my way inside. I cross the room and pull it closed. I check the drying meat. Next to the kitchen window is the dehydration rack. Four strips of ray meat are missing and the small kitchen window is broken.

My days never begin with such strange occurrences.

—

I spend my day prying the broken kitchen window out of its frame with iron and wooden tools. Then I spend the other half of the day prying the kitchen window out of a vacant house on the edge of the settlement. The machines didn't make all of the houses exactly the same; some of the measurements are off. The new window is five millimeters too short on either side. I head to the north where there is a stockpile of dried Hevea that I've been collecting. I walk there with hatchet in hand and shake off the strange sensation of being watched. The last time that tremor zipped down my spine was the last teacher was watching me gut a yellow-ringed barracuda with a large knife when I was eight—it was a test to see if I could handle the gore and the wicked blade. I keep walking until the sensation fades.

The moon grass is tall on this side of the settlement. Pale green and nearly yellow, it tickles the fingertips of my free hand. My teachers said that the grass and trees grow taller here due to the low gravity and their search for sunlight.

The wood is stored in a shed with corroded walls, stacked high to the ceiling from years of collection and disuse. I collect four narrow, meter long logs, secure them under my arm, and head back.

The ground under my feet grumbles as the crust of the moon shifts, a typical occurrence when a sister-moon is near. The gas giant is in its regular place in the sky, and a sister-moon has entered the backdrop. In the distance I hear the tide of the yellow sea and I become aggravated. I've lost a day hunting with repairing this window. While the gardens still grow a variety of vegetables, it's not enough protein for survival. Today was my day to collect the dainty mussels that grow along the base of the sandbar.

After the window is fixed, I collect the broken glass in a bucket and leave it near the door with the plan of fashioning the sharp shards into cutting tools. I check on the drying ray skin, stretch it tight and secure it on the drying rack. I go inside and check the remaining strips of meat. With a stained strip of cloth I clean the dried blood and small specks of glass from the counter. I resalt the meat and check it for glass. I'm careful to avoid injury since the last doctor died when I was twelve. A gut full of glass will get me nothing but a slow death.

After draining the last jug of fresh water, I collect the empty jugs and head for the atmospheric water generator. The settlement has twenty of them placed three hundred meters apart through the center of the settlement. There were plans to place one in every household but there wasn't time for that. The original settlers were ingrained with the know-how of technology, unfortunately that knowledge wasn't passed on to the right children, those who were meant to develop more perished before they had time to build anything. Death seems to be the curse of my moon.

The generators draw fresh water out of the local humid atmosphere. I've never thirsted a day since birth, besides that time when I explored the other side of the moon. The dryness and heat parched my throat and I drained my water jugs in half the time I had meant them to last.

The closest water generator to my home is a forty-meter walk, one of the few paths worn down by my own feet from filling my jugs every few days. The shiny contraption was built out of stainless steel acquired from the Colony ship. I set my first jug under the spout. I open the nozzle and wait. Nothing comes out. This is strange. In twenty-seven years I've never once had this water generator go dry. The grass under the spout is damp, the soil as well. It's as though I—since I am the only one here—lay underneath the spout to bathe and drink my fill without regard. I would never do such a thing. Or would I? Who else is here to do it? Unable to come up with a rational excuse in my mind, I collect my jugs and walk the three hundred meters to the next one.

—

I wake from a steady sleep, one induced by absence of previous night's rest and physical exhaustion. I eat a solid meal of dried ray meat, softened grains, and raw legumes. Back to the task of the wet suit, I find the new one and try it on. It seems to fit good enough. The natural rubber stretches to accommodate my long limbs. I decide to take it for a test run in the sea.

This morning the front door is latched, just as I left it before bed. I open the door, turn to close it tight. When I turn again I notice that the ray skin is gone from its drying rack.

Damnit.

The grass is undisturbed near the drying rack, but with the low gravity it never stays patted down for long. The wind could have taken the skin, but I don't remember hearing the wind howling in the night. I was sleeping heavily. Something could have taken it but nothing has left the sea. I know that nothing has evolved to leave the sea. Unless it has…

I twist my face to the sky and check the atmosphere. The air could be thick with volcanic ash, it could be affecting my reasoning, wouldn't be the first time it's happened here. Three generations ago there was a mass die off after fourteen of the moon-volcanoes ejected thick ash into the heavens. A near-darkness settled on the population, famine and wild behavior struck, moon-maddness my mother called it. If they didn't starve, they killed themselves and their loved ones, fearing eternal darkness. I thought I was immune. There have been days of high volcanic activity, when the ground below my feet rumbled for hours on end. The ash never seemed to affect me before but something strange is happening now.

The ray skin is lost, as well as the opportunity for a new pair of shoes. I glance down at my feet; I'll have to wait. I scrub my hands over my face, blink a few times and shake my head. Perhaps the curse that killed my ancestors is coming for me.

I make my way to the sea. A swim will cure my mind. Maybe I'll catch another ray. And possibly I will exit the yellow sea renewed, refreshed, and with a clear head. That is all I truly need today.

The walk is not leisurely, since I am eager to prove… Wait, who am I going to prove anything to? Do I need to prove it to myself? I should prove it to myself. These strange things that have been happening, there's only so many reasons for why. I am not one of my ancestral scientists who droned on and on with their theories of this and that and blah, blah, blah, blah. No, I am a survivor. But, it would be nice to exit the water alleviated of my current predicaments.

Sometimes I stand on the edge of the shore and let the golden water lap at my feet as I scan the horizon and map my swimming path. The shelf drop off is severe two-hundred meters out, there's a sand bar to the left which is good for collecting crabs and snails, to the right is another deep drop where I hunt for the rays.

This day I don't wait to map out my path, I run into the sea, arms pumping, knees to chest until I'm out of breath and I reach the shelf. I swim past the shelf drop off, tread water for enough time to fill my lungs with air, then I dive deep. The water is murky, gets clearer as it gets deeper. A school of tiny silver fish swims by me. I claw at the water and drag myself deeper, eager to run from the strangeness on the surface. The steep drop off of the shelf becomes an angled seafloor. I search the sand for the beady eyes of a moon-ray, eager to replace the missing skin and meat that seems to have disappeared. I worry that perhaps I've hunted them into extinction. I stretch my arms. At least the new suit is holding up. The seams haven't stretched or separated.

The pressure changes around me, something is swimming near. The movement is swirling. I still, settle my feet on the seafloor and search the water around me. The water turns murky again; whatever beast is nearby is disturbing the sand. The pressure pattern alters from something swimming nearby to closing in on me. The worst creatures of the sea are the moon-barracudas, the stinging jellyfish, sea snakes, and something that looks suspiciously similar to an earthen crocodile. Most of those creatures don't come this close to the sea shelf, they hunt further out in waters less explored, where I know the docile fish are larger and greater populated. Something *thumps* against my back. It circles me. I blink, trying to catch a glimpse but the sand is too thick. *Thump*, it slaps me in the chest. I would prefer a quick death but not one suffocating on the sea floor, foolishly I did not come prepared with a hook or a rope or a knife. I thrust my feet off of the sand and propel myself towards the surface. At first, the water pressure around my body does not change, the sand still thick, and I cannot see. But then, the creature slides across my left arm. It's a leisurely movement, as though it's teasing, giving itself time to explore me and I it. I can tell it's large, sleekly muscled and fast. And then, deciding to get a real taste of me, I feel the searing burn as a jagged tooth slices across my arm. Perhaps deciding it didn't like the taste of human, the flank of the creature slides across my wound, then, with a goodbye kiss it flicks me with its large tailfin.

I roll in the sea, head over heels. Trying to figure out which way is up, my head feeling ready to explode from too much time under the surface. I pull my arms in and let the last of the air escape my lungs, the bubbles show me which way to swim. I swim up, frantic, using both of my arms, fearing that the unknown sea beast might return and gobble me whole. I break the surface, gasping and coughing, the yellow sea surrounding me swirling with blood. I hold up my injured arm and examine the cut. It's deep, across the length of my forearm.

—

Water drips down my body as I make my way out of the sea. I hold my arm, blood dripping over my fingertips, leaving orange droplets after mixing with the sand. The bite hurts worse than anything I've ever experienced.

As I'm nearing the beach, I shake the water out of my hair. The droplets hover in the air for a moment, the low gravity giving them the chance to rise to the atmosphere if they'd like. I bat the droplets away, urge them back to the sea. I need them there. I need the sea. I need—

There's an indent in the sand near my foot. Oblong, a curved center, five tiny dots across the top. I step next to it, lift my foot from the sand and examine the print left behind. Is it a tiny human footprint? In an instant both prints are washed away by the tide. I shake my head, close my eyes only to open them again and find a figure standing on the beach with me.

It's a girl. Not a young girl. She looks to be about the same age as me. Her eyes are large, full pupils with a faint ring of blue. Her eyes are not like the people before me. Her eyes are just like mine.

Whatever beast was in the sea must have been venomous, this girl nothing but a hallucination caused by the poison.

"Who are you?" I ask.

"Who are *you*?" she replies.

Do hallucinations speak back? She looks scared, like she's seen a ghost or something she didn't expect.

"How did you get here?" I ask.

"How did *you* get here?"

"What are you doing here?"

She doesn't respond.

Fearing that I've completely lost my mind, conversing with a figment of my imagination that refuses to answer my questions, I say, "This is my moon. I demand you answer me!" I've never raised my voice and the bellowing demand scares what's left of the lonely boy inside of me.

Her mouth snaps shut and she takes a few steps backward.

"Wait!" I reach out with a bloody hand. Do I want her to go? I don't want her to go. This is the first person I've seen in nearly two decades. I decide I don't want her to go, even if she is a ghost or a moon-mirage or a venom-induced hallucination. "Please. Don't go. What's your name?"

She blinks. "Jupiter."

"Jupiter… Jupiter. Jupiter. Jupiter. *Jupiter*," I find myself mumbling. Her name is a song on my lips. Fresh and new, yet, familiar. "Fifth planet from the sun." Not the sun in the distance, the sun from where we originated.

"That is my name. And you are?" She tilts her head to the side.

"Kale."

At first she seems shocked, then an ease rolls through her small body as though I am an old friend whom she simply didn't recognize. "Ah." She smiles. "It was only a matter of time before we found each other. You are my moon."

Found each other? Who is this? Must be a figment of my imagination. I glance to the sky again. The gas giant hangs suspended in place; the ice rings in their home across the skyline. There is no thickness of ash, there is no reasoning for hallucinations. Maybe it was the ray meat? I touch my mouth, remember the things I've eaten the past few days. There was nothing new. Unless the rays have evolved. They could be emitting a toxin. That could explain this. My arm throbs. Or it could be the sea creature bite. All it took was the slice of a jagged tooth to bring the angel of death to me.

"Kale?"

I blink.

Jupiter's smile is soft and sweet. I suddenly notice the curve to her hips, the length of dark hair cascading down her back, full breasts—

"Are you done?"

I snap out of it. "I can't help it. Been a very long time since I've seen a female." I cross my arms to ensure I don't reach out to touch her. My eyes drop to the colorful material secured around her waist. Wait. "Is that—"

"My people need help," she interrupts.

"Your people?"

"Kale." She starts to walk backward. "You should probably change into something more suitable for the darkside of the moon."

"There's nothing on the darkside."

"Are you so sure?"

I follow her.

There's nothing on the other side, just a violent landscape. I searched as far as I could see. I went to explore during that time of darkness when I wanted more than just the lonely existence I'd become accustomed to. I searched for someone, for something, anything. All I found was bubbling lava and sulfur fields.

"There's nothing there."

"I've been there. My people are there. And we need your help."

She leads me down the beaten path to my home as though she's been there before. We pass rows of iron houses, stopping at my own. Jupiter opens the front door and lets herself in. I follow.

"Don't forget that you're bleeding." She motions to my arm.

I glance down. "Yes." I swallow, feeling a bit sick. "I'll be right back." I walk to short distance to the bathroom, close the door and strip the top portion of my wetsuit off. I guess the injury doesn't look so bad. It still burns. Infection and the possibility of venom worry me. I wash the wound and wrap it with a long strip of sterilized cloth, then I wash the blood off my hands. I've never had an injury that's leaked this much blood before.

I leave the bathroom in search of clean clothing in my bedroom. I change out of the wetsuit and into my normal clothing, sure that when I open the door again there will be nothing but an empty room.

Jupiter is still standing in the kitchen, eating a strip of ray meat.

"Strange how much better this tastes after it's cured for more time," she says.

I walk across the room. "You broke in the other night."

"I did."

"You stole from me."

"I was hungry." She takes another strip of meat. "I couldn't just knock on the door and ask for some porridge. What if you were a murderer?"

"What's porridge?" I ask. "It sounds terrible."

Jupiter shrugs. "I've never had it before." She taps the side of her head. "A wealth of knowledge with minimal experience." She glances at me, up and down.

"And a murderer?" I ask.

"People who kill their own kind."

"There have been murders here, ages ago."

"Is that why you are alone?" She seems suddenly serious. "Where are the rest of your people?"

"The moon killed them. Not me. I simply held their hands during their last breaths and buried them by the mountains."

"How long have you been alone?" she asks.

"Since I was a child." I blink a few times, cautiously relieved when she is still there.

"That is a long time to be alone."

"I know this. But I am not a murderer, and I have no porridge to offer you."

Jupiter nods as though I've passed a test. She moves away from the counter. "Are you ready?" She walks to the door and holds it open, waiting for me.

—

Jupiter leads me across the jagged ridges of silicate rock, across the protective horseshoe that I have called home for all of my natural life, a place of safety, security. I ventured out before but swore never to attempt again. But that was before her.

She never tires, never stops to catch her breath or take a drink. I slow behind her, guzzle water after an hour. By the time we descend the mountain I am dripping with sweat. Before us, there is a gray shift in the light. The darkside is there. Threatening and strange, just as frightening as the first time I felt its loom, but I was nothing more than a child then, easily scared. All those years ago, I never had a moon-mirage to guide me.

The ground rumbles with volcanic activity, the pole-stretching sulfur sea threatens with waves and sea-spray. Jupiter walks straight for it. I follow, anticipating her to change direction. She doesn't. She steps directly into the dark and violent water.

I grab her arm. "It's not safe," I warn. "The sea will swallow you up whole and spit you out a volcano."

She taps her foot down. "It's shallow. All the way across."

"Shallow?" I step into the water beside her. There is no continental shelf to drop me off into the depths of the sea, only firm sand underneath my feet.

I follow her across a shallow sea. One I've never explored alone, but have avoided due to its rash nature. For hundreds and hundreds of meters, the water only brims to our calves and knees.

Before us there's a cluster of jagged mountains, similar to the alcove I live in.

"There," Jupiter points to the ridge, "just over those rocks."

Jupiter picks up her pace, seawater swirling around her legs, threatening to tug her to deeper waters but never successful.

My clothing is soaked, my injured arm aching, my mind blown by the fact that I feared the darkside for so many years. Fear won. I never took the chance to explore further.

The water shallows to a coarse and elemental crusted beach. There is a rough path through the mountain, which, up close, seems like more of a large and sharp hillside. It seemed daunting those years ago, towering above my head.

Her legs are red from traipsing across the sea, her feet scratched and raw. I am nearly overcome by the sudden urge to hunt a hundred rays and use the skin to fashion her protective boots and pants.

"There," Jupiter points.

A ship is smoldering in the valley. Dark outlines of more people are scattered about. The alcove fills with their dull chatter of planning and preparing.

"We've lost many," she says.

This is my moon. I've sworn to protect it against another Colony. I swore to stop another Colony. I've feared the recklessness my ancestors brought to earth; never want that to touch this land.

I feel pressure on my arm. She's touching me. When was the last time I felt touch? Over fifteen years ago, the day my father died. The day I buried the last of my people and last touch I felt was that of a corpse. Jupiter's is different, soft and firm and… *alive*. To go so long without that contact, I want to pull her close, tug her body against mine and bury my face in her hair, make up for the lost years of feeling no other's skin but my own.

"Will you help us?" Jupiter asks.

My response takes minutes. My jaw slack, mind racing. It's now or never. Help her, help people like me, or end them. Go back to the silence, the alone, those dark moments of gripping fear threatening to end me like it did the people decades ago. I don't want to die of moon-maddness. I don't want to die alone. I want to *belong*.

These people will die on the darkside of my moon. The Earthen stories are too easy to remember though. This moon can sustain a small population, no more. I can't risk more being sent.

"First, we have to destroy the AI, we have to destroy Colony." Jupiter nods, starts to walk away. I grab her arm. "Wait. How did you become like me?" I motion to my eyes.

"It altered the genome. Adjusted the DNA in our chromosomes with what biological chemicals the AI had on board." She points to the smoldering ship. "Made many of us like you. The rest," she motions to the flames, "it killed them off, knew they wouldn't survive long here. The rationale was that they'd be a waste of resources." Her eyes are glossy. She wipes away a tear. "I never knew them but it just seems so wrong."

I nearly forgot the stories of the vat-raised primary colony. I had heard that the AI imprinted education and interaction straight into the human brain. I have never heard of the technology to change the genome.

"We can't risk this happening again," I say. "I've lived through one extinction already. They can't send more." My arm throbs suddenly, reminding me of the fact that if infection sets in I may not be around to avoid another extinction much longer.

"I know."

Jupiter's eyes are large and glossy, her chin quivers. Her bicep twitches under my hand. I remember her words, *you are my moon*. Did she already know of me? How could she know of me? I have avoided the original Colony lander, avoided the AI just as my father warned. Perhaps his speculation of it being too late was correct, perhaps the AI had already communicated with the satellites and called another settlement.

—

Jupiter doesn't know the names of her people. She's just met them herself a few days before she came searching for me. There are ninety-five survivors, birthed from a ship at the whim of an AI who tampered with the genome. Everyone introduces himself or herself. Some are highly educated, some largely muscled and brute. They all speak to a field of expertise: doctors, scientists, farmers, metal workers, those skilled in technologies of earth. Strangely, they seem to recognize me before I introduce myself.

We scavenge for supplies, taking anything that we can carry and that might be of use. And then torch the place. The Colony lander smokes and fumes.

"Where are your tractors and drilling machines?" I ask, curious.

"They would have arrived here before us. Nearly thirty years ago."

The understanding is strong; they have been there for years. Eggs in vats, hiding on the darkside of my moon. Colony holding them, waiting for the genetic data to modify them for survival on the moon, maybe even to put false memories of me in their brains.

"The tractors and diggers should be working now," Jupiter says.

They could be working, if I hadn't directed them straight into the lava pits.

Jupiter and I lead the people across the mountain, across the sea and away from the darkside. They seem worried as we cross the sulfur sand dunes, mesmerized as the sand spins suspended by the wind, and when we cross the silicate mountains that lead to my iron and glass village, they gasp with joy.

The people pick their own dwellings; there are enough for everyone to have three. I show them the water purifiers, the gardens at the back of the settlement, the yellow sea where I catch my prey.

The doctor inspects my injured arm and assures me that it will not bring death. Jupiter is by my side the entire time. She smiles softly when the doctor presses his fingers to my neck and under my arms.

"Checking your lymph nodes," he tells me. "You're strong. You'll heal up just fine." With a pat on the shoulder he walks away.

When the tour is over, and the exhausted people take off on their own to explore and learn, to make this moon their home, I turn to Jupiter. She looks lovely with the gas giant as her halo.

"You are no longer alone, moon lord." She touches my chest, her small hand over my heartbeat.

"This is not some fever or the moon-maddness coming to take my life?" I want her to promise me. I need to be sure.

"How would you know?" Jupiter's hands move to my shoulders. "Would it be so bad?" She asks. "For me to be the moon-death, leading you away as I did your ancestors?"

It would not disappoint me to die in the arms of another. It would, after all, be my turn. As a young boy I held many as they passed. More than I fear the volcanoes and the lava, I fear a death of solitude.

"Are you?" I ask. She could be death. Or in a nauseating twist of fate I could be the one floating in a vat, the AI toying with my brain, training me for a hard lived life.

The warmth of her hands is distracting. I look away, towards the gas giant and the ice rings and the sister-moon about to pass by.

"Kale." Her soft hand touches my chin, refocuses my eyes on hers.

I wrap my arms across her back. I've never held a woman in my embrace before. She stretches up on her toes, hesitates for a split second before pressing her precious lips to mine. Jupiter's kiss. Supernovae explode behind my eyelids, blindingly bright. Galaxies wink and glint at a seizure inducing pace. Nebulas burst, spiral and plume, their dust of rust and deep purples and royals blues more mesmerizing than any earth rainbow.

She pulls away.

I open my eyes. She feels real under my palms, her body firm and warm. As I hold her, I come to the realization that I've only been surviving. In each day that I've spent harvesting and hunting, I was merely going through the motions of life. This is the most alive I've felt in the seventeen years since my father died. The buzzing chatter of new settlers exploring their homes behind me is more soothing than I ever expected it would be.

"You are *my* moon," Jupiter promises.

Alive, dying, or mad, I'll take it. I'll take every ounce of it. After all, what good is survival if you're surviving alone?

Asteroid Riders

"Which one did you pick?" First Officer Jack asks.

The asteroid belt looms before us and an interactive screen layered over the window labels each asteroid that passes. Each is assigned final coordinates for proper placement in the creation of the moon. The computer displays an interlocking puzzle all of the asteroids on a loop. All of the asteroid riders have been watching it for days, trying to get a feel for what rock we want and a plan for the ride.

"That one." I point at asteroid 552Mendoza.

"I wanted that one." He flashes a charming smile that doesn't hint at our tepid past.

"Of course you did." I have to force a smile, one that feels connected to my heart and tugs it to the center of my throat.

I could choke on my feelings for Jack.

Damn the memories that I have of him before all of this.

I'll let him take the largest, most out of control asteroid in the belt. He deserves it. Perfect rock for a First Officer. Anyone attempting to blast-maneuver an asteroid the size of a dwarf planet off its orbit and out of the belt, either has a death wish or significant brain injury. I glance at him. I vote for brain injury. He's too vain for a death wish. I know that first hand.

There are twenty-seven asteroids that have been selected for the second moon of Phaeton. 247Saratov, three kilometers in radius and comprised mostly of iron, is lit up in red, which means it's available. I tap on one of the smaller asteroids, 315Angarsk, it's metal-type, approximately the diameter of a small town at seventeen kilometers, oblong with large pockmarks on its surface. This will be the equivalent of riding a giant tortoise across space. I glance at the asteroid Jack chose and decide I'll pick a tortoise over riding a giant Ankylosaurus any day. At least I can run across 315Angarsk, Jack is going to have to take a grav-rover, which could be dangerous. If the rover breaks down and the rider can't place their thrusters and magnet in time, the entire mission is at stake.

I glance at Jack's biceps bulging from his skintight UnderArmour; he can handle it. Big strong guy like that can handle just about anything.

"You're not still mad, are you, Nat?"

"Why would I be mad?" I bite my cheeks to keep my face expressionless.

Jack drops his voice. "I just don't want what happened between us to impact the mission. There's a lot riding on the outcome of this. Your officer rank—"

"Just stop." I can't believe him.

"Nat—"

"It's Second Officer Natalie to you. Especially on the helm."

"Whoa." Jack's hands rise, palms out, in a calming gesture. "I know how you women get up here. Floating around in space gets your hormones off-kilter. That's how they said the other one died."

"Jesus. She didn't die because of hormones. Amber was killed during an accident in the making of the first moon."

She was my friend and we all felt the guilt of her death. None of us could save her.

"They said she got too emotional."

I can't tell if he's being sarcastic or not.

"She was crushed between two giant rocks when her thrusters malfunctioned," I say.

"Quiet, Officers!" the Captain scolds.

We're not supposed to talk about Amber, especially not moments before our next mission.

Bad for morale, the Captain warned before we left Earth.

Jack's face is flexed in concern as he whispers, "Just be careful out there. I know what happened before, with us, I know it can make you *edgy*."

"That's not exactly how I'd categorize it." Murderous maybe, not edgy. Emotions run high on the edge of the galaxy.

"Come on. You're supposed to forgive me."

"Can't do that."

"You're not playing by the rules." He crosses his arms over his chest, the movement makes his pecs and biceps bulge. I think he does that on purpose, trying to distract me.

"Rules?" I lick my lips and look away.

"Rider-bylaw C12.7894 appendix Z, all riders must formally forgive wrongdoings in conscious effort to ensure continued teamwork."

Hm. Don't remember that. Truth be told it sounds like bull-crap. I'm over this conversation. "Happy riding, Jack-hole."

"Don't be like that, Nat. I said I was sorry."

Sorry doesn't cut it when you walk in on your boyfriend with his pants around his ankles, bending a shipmaid over a barrel and showing her the big dipper. Not twenty-four hours earlier he had proposed marriage.

I walk away from First Officer Jack, following 315Angarsk on its orbit. My fingers hover over the holo-screen, itching to claim it. My first asteroid ride was about half the size of this one. That rock was small, like driving a Matchbox car, and I was afraid I was going to fall for most of the mission. I parked that sucker in the tiniest cranny of the first moon, nearly lost my fingers when the magnet powered up causing the edges of the rock to slide and crumble against the bordering asteroids. Training doesn't prepare you for the shock of the magnets kicking into action, thought I lost every molar in my head.

Someone walks up behind me. Afraid that they'll claim Angarsk, I tap the screen. The asteroid dims, signaling it's been claimed. Relief rushes me. The biggest decision of the day is finally over.

"Natalie?" a familiar voice asks.

I turn. It's Nick, a guy I met in college and then again in wrangler-school. He'd been chosen for the first moon creation but after renegades tried to disrupt our mission by poisoning the food, Nick didn't get his turn to ride an asteroid. He was too busy purging the devil from every orifice after eating Chilean Sea Bass that had been garnished with a heaping of shigellosis.

Thus, my one rule to live by: never eat seafood in space.

"I didn't know you were on this tour." I hug him—it's hard not to when you've survived wrangler-school together. "When did you dock?"

"A few hours ago. Just long enough to grab dinner and send a message home to mom."

"I'm so glad to see you." And I am. Nick is just one of those guys, easy to get along with and pleasant. Plus, it's a good distraction not having to think about Jack.

Turning back to the screen, I ask, "Which one did you choose?"

He points at 753Qingdao.

"A Chinese asteroid?"

"What's that matter? You chose Russian."

"Maybe I'm one-quarter Russian." I press my lips together to hold in a smile.

"Maybe I'm one-quarter Chinese." Nick walks closer and bends so he's face to face with me. "Or maybe you work for the Russian government and you just want them to own a higher stake in the second moon."

"They did promise me a lifetime supply of vodka." I run my tongue across my front teeth. "And gold incisors if I succeeded."

A moment of silence passes before Nick says, "You're so full of shit."

I laugh. "You're right. I wanted to go a little bigger than my last ride. This one caught my attention. And, you know, if there's one thing you learn in wrangler-school, it's to go with your gut instinct."

"That's what they say." Nick glances behind me. "So what's up with him?" He tilts his chin in Jack's direction.

"History." I shake my head. "I don't want to think about Jack right now. I'm trying to focus on this ride."

Nick is staring at the asteroid field. "Speaking of history. Never thought we'd end up here. Not after where we started."

I follow his gaze to the giant planet looming just beyond the asteroid belt. Humans successfully created a planet between the orbit of Mars and Jupiter using the Asteroid Collection Method. They named it Phaeton. Heinrich Olbers probably rolled over in his grave the day the planet was named. Fancy machines and a few thousand brave souls are terraforming at an impressive pace. Word is that the new planet will be ready for it's first arrival of refugees from Earth in less than a year.

The Asteroid field is a third of what it used to be. The thousands of bits of flying rock were used to make Phaeton, and now we're making moons with the scraps that have been left behind. The satellites will be enhancing tidal forces on the new planet and providing extra surface area for the human population to spread. There are glossy posters in the mess hall, propaganda from Earth promising an alien planet with three or more moons, ice rings, sulfur clouds and next closest galaxy better visible in the night sky. The skyscape is impressive, the artwork spectacular.

"There are only nine left for choosing," Nick warns.

The last riders are selecting their asteroids and memorizing their strategic maneuvers for a carbonaceous, silicate, or metallic rock. 490Ningbo has been chosen. 895Alaska dims, followed by 776Montana, then 033Quebec, 331Chuhuahua, 934Brisbane, 903Athens, 882Barcelona, and 994Kolkata all dim. A tone sounds across the ship, signaling that each rider has chosen an asteroid. Some will be smaller than mine, many larger, Jack having chosen the largest and most dangerous of them all.

"That's all she wrote," Nick mutters.

"Prepare for departure," the Captain announces.

The ship is suddenly a flurry of activity.

We begin donning our spacesuits. I bend to tie my boots. They're heavy, thick and steel-toed, designed to protect and anchor. The work we do is labor intensive and dangerous, a stubbed toe could be the end all. I clip my grav-belt, my fingers trembling with the memory of how fast the thrusters force the asteroids to move. In just a few hours I'll be skipping across the galaxy on a chunk of rock at nearly three hundred kilometers per hour.

Getting my left hand glove on is always the hardest part. I've got the thing wedged between my knees and I'm trying to shove my hand in while pulling on the material with the bulky fingertips of my right hand.

"Let me help you with that," Jack is at my side.

"I can do it."

"We both know better." He pulls the glove from between my knees and holds it out, waiting.

I push my hand in.

"Be safe out there," he says, his voice low.

"I did just fine last time."

"Don't forget rule number one."

"Never leave your asteroid."

"Don't die." His tone is grim, concerned.

We line up near the bay door. Twenty-six men, one woman. Jack is at the front of the line. He turns and winks at me before stepping into the airlock. Through the thick transparent divider we can see everything going on out there. The crew checks his gear, cinches his straps, and knocks on his helmet.

Jack reaches up and tests the zip-line above his head. Essentially, it's a zip-line of near death. The asteroid rider rappels to their rock, followed by a container of gear. The rider will be equipped with enough pulse-thrusters and maneuvering-thrusters to navigate the asteroid out of orbit. There will be a giant magnet and rock-hammer to pound it into the asteroid, and duct tape. Rolls and rolls of duct tape. A wise man once said that duct tape should be worshiped. It's one of the few inventions of Earth that still has use today. There are loads of it on every ship. I used an entire roll of it to secure a hole in my suit during the making of the first moon as I was floating in space waiting for recovery.

We pick up speed. The high tensile line shoots out of the ship and embeds itself into the asteroid 552Mendoza. The hatch door opens. The crew secures him to the line then Jack slaps his chest, setting off one of his thrusters. He zooms out of the ship. Next they send a chest of gear and a grav-rover. His rock will have more gravity than the rest of ours so he doesn't need as many lines and tethers, but he's still traveling with a lot of crap.

I hold my breath, my eyes locked on Jack's back. I wanted nothing more than to cause him severe bodily harm a few moments ago but right now I just want him to reach 552Mendoza without losing an arm or a leg or his life. The man can get on my last nerve but I just can't shake him.

Soon Jack is nothing but a spec in space.

The twenty-six asteroid riders left in line change their focus to the ship's screens where we watch Jack's progress from his helmet-cam. Tiny asteroids no bigger than my fist pass in front of his face. 552Mendoza is in front of him. He's moving fast, hundreds of kilometers an hour. There's a *thud* and whistle of air as he tries to slow himself with his thrusters. He slaps it twice before he gets enough resistance. 552Mendoza is right there, filling the screen with its massiveness.

My gut sinks. I'd never try to ride a rock that big. Too much risk.

"I can feel her gravity," Jack announces across his comm. "This is good. We're good here."

We all hear him in our helmets. All of the asteroid riders can communicate with each other and the ship.

Numbers tick and calculate on the ship's screen as the computer analyzes data from 552Mendoza. I don't know exactly what the machine calculates since we are the brunt and not the brains. We've been taught how to ride the asteroid, not the pure science of melding them together. Only know that you have to jump off that sucker before the center magnet performs some magic that creates a core and solidifies all the bits of asteroid together.

Jack lands on his feet, shoots a tether into the crust of 552Mendoza and secures himself before turning and securing another tether a two meters away. The next few minutes are tense. Jack has to tether his gear that's flying down the zip-line toward his asteroid, then cut the line so the ship can retract it.

Dust bursts as he blasts a third tether into the ground beneath his feet. The box of gear is barreling towards him. *Pfft*. He hits it with a tether that loops around the four sides of the box, cinches it tight and secures it. *Pfft*. He hits the rover and secures it. He cuts the line and the ship alters speed for the next rider's departure.

My eyes are glued to the screen, watching Jack as the gravity of 552Mendoza secures the container of gear and the rover against its crust. The asteroid is so large that it looks like he's already walking on a moon.

"Next up!" the Captain announces.

Second Officer Charlie is the next rider to step into the airlock. He chose 033Quebec. The ship's screen illuminates as we get closer to the asteroid. The crew secures him to the zip-line. The hatch opens and Charlie zooms out.

It's the same with Second Officers Zack, Bob, Chuck, and the rest of the riders. Until it's my turn.

My palms are sweating under the thick material of my gloves. The air-lock opens. I step through. The crew checks over my suit to ensure everything is secured properly. They pack gear into a bag, fasten tools and more equipment to my suit. A computerized voice counts down in my helmet. 315Angarsk is a kilometer away. The zip-line shoots out. My heart thuds heavily. Panic and excitement war within my chest. They clip me to the line. I lift my heels, a bit too short to test the line with my feet flat on the deck of the ship.

"… one… go," the ship's computer ends the countdown.

The hatch opens.

The suction of space and force of my suit thrusters send me flying out of the ship. Soaring through the cosmos, there is epic silence all around me. The only feeling of gravity being that of my pressure suit. I nearly forgot how this feels; adrift, anchorless. I am nothing but a spec in the universe. The hazy white clouds of the Milky Way and the rust and lavender clouds of more galaxies beyond are spectacular. I have never felt so small. Focusing on the spiral galaxies in the distance, I wonder if the beings over there have ever felt this?

The comm in my helmet is silent, the crew awaiting my assessment of 315Angarsk. I ignite my suit's forward thrusters to slow my speed, grab onto the line and tilt my body so my feet land steady on Angarsk. The case of supplies is barreling down the line. I shoot a tether to catch it before cutting the zip-line.

"We're good here," I announce to the crew.

The ship moves on to the next drop. I am alone.

—

"Hey, Nat?" Jack's voice breaks through the chatter of twenty-seven riders talking to themselves and the ship.

"What?" I'm drilling a hole to place the magnet at the tip of 315Angarsk.

"Did you land okay?"

"Just fine."

"How's 315Angarsk treating you?"

"Well the rock hasn't lied to me yet, so I'd say so far so good."

"We really should talk about it." His rover engine whines in the background. He must be placing his blast-thrusters. He's going to need a hell of a lot of force to knock that asteroid off of its orbit.

"Nothing to talk about." The hole is complete. I secure the drill and reach for giant magnet, settling the stem of it into place.

"I still have feelings for you. What I said before was true. I'm sorry."

I slam my hammer. "Are we on a private line?" The last thing I need is every rider listening to this.

It's embarrassing enough that most of them know the details.

"It's private," he assures me.

"You broke my goddamned heart. And now you want forgiveness?"

"Not everything is what you think. After we created the first moon, I felt invincible. Hell, I felt like a God. Women were throwing themselves at me left and right."

"You think men weren't doing the same to me?"

"It's different with women."

"How?"

There's a beat of silence before he suggests, "Maybe we should talk about this when we get back to Earth."

Time to break the news to him. "I'm not going back to Earth. I'm not going back, Jack. And if you want to try and work this thing out it's going to take a helluva lot more than a confession while I'm in the middle of riding an asteroid. Rider bylaw XA76.2G, don't distract your fellow rider with personal shit while they're trying to focus on the task at hand."

"You just made that up."

"No I didn't." I grip my hammer harder.

"You always make stuff up when it suits you, like that ridiculous story you told me about meeting the President of the International Space Committee."

"I actually met the man and have a picture of him shaking my hand."

"I've never seen it."

"You never asked to see it. I didn't make it up."

"I know you did."

I give up. "Whatever, sure, I made it up. Just like your marriage proposal."

"That wasn't—"

"I'm out. Private line off." The chatter of the other riders returns.

I slam the hammer down hard, imagining I'm pounding Jack's handsome face, until the magnet is in place and secure. I get off my knees, my boots landing heavy on the ground as I make my way to place the maneuvering-thrusters. It's solitary work, every rider doing the same thing on his or her own rock. I traverse the diameter of 315Angarsk in a few hours' time and secure the thrusters, along the edges and the bottom of my asteroid. After, I check my data pad, synch the thrusters and review the flight plan.

I sit on my asteroid for the next few hours of travel. It's the perfect time to reflect. Some of the finest musings of mankind have been created under the pressure of the stars. Strangely, I can think of nothing at this time. I guess that's what happens when you need to rearrange your life but don't want to move on.

"Hey, Natalie?" Nick's voice breaks through and he doesn't sound good.

"What's wrong? You didn't eat the Sea Bass, did you?"

"Shrimp Scampi."

"Jesus. Never eat the seafood! You should know better."

"But it smelled so good." There's a thud and sharp whoosh of air. "Something's wrong with my thrusters. They're not synching with my data pad."

"Did you try manual override?"

"Three times." He lets loose a string of curse words.

"You'll have to manually do it." This could get dangerous, but we've been trained for moments like this. "What's the diameter of your rock?"

"Forty-two kilometers."

"How fast can you run?"

"Officially?"

I am silent. *Officially…*

"Private line," he requests.

"You cheated on your qualifying physical?"

"It's a long story."

Jesus. This just keeps getting better.

"Natalie?"

"I'm here. How far are you from me?"

"A few clicks. If I stand on a ridge I can see you at my two o'clock. And I can see Second Officer Bob working on his rock at ten o'clock."

I check my gear. There are enough extra tethers to try what I'm thinking.

Nick is a white speck on a giant flying rock. He's waving his arms. "Can you see me?"

"I see you."

"What are you doing?" he asks.

"Something I'm not supposed to do."

We can't abandon the asteroid, the second moon requires it. I couldn't help Amber but I can help him. I ignite a thruster and knock my rock off of its orbit a few hours too soon. My data pad erupts with red blinking lights and alarms.

"Second Officer Natalie!" the Captain's voice erupts in my helmet. "What in the hell are you doing?"

"We've got a situation. Nick's thrusters aren't working."

"We are well aware and on it. He's number twelve in line for assistance.

"ETA of assistance?" I ask.

"Two hours," the Captain replies. He sounds determined, but he knows just as well as I do that we don't have two hours to spare. We'll be to Phaeton in less time than that, and nearing our final destination. Fearing a fate similar to Amber's for Nick, I take action.

I reprogram my data pad and thrusters. A thruster bursts and angles my asteroid so it's heading for 753Qingdao.

"Please tell me your magnet is in place?"

"It is," he replies.

"Thank God."

I'm not a scientist but I played with magnets as a kid. There's force and attraction. I'm hoping the magnets that we pound into the front of our asteroids have the same properties.

When Nick's rock is so close I could reach out and touch it, I shoot the tethers and anchor our asteroids together. The magnets engage. Rock crunches and crumbles as the two asteroids rub against each other.

Nick is running across his rock, nearly soaring in the low gravity. At least the thrusters on his suite are working. "You are going to get in so much trouble," he warns as he slows in front of me.

I move, crossing my rock to pound one of the thrusters out of my asteroid. I secure it in the pocket of my space suit, and then I start running.

"What are you doing?" Nick asks.

"Replacing yours."

I run faster than I've ever run in my life. Running in low gravity with these heavy boots is almost like running on sand. Jack took me to the beach once when we were training for the building of the first-moon. He warned me what it would be like, gave me tips to help. I hate him for not always being a complete asshole.

The thruster is flashing on the edge of Nick's rock. I kick it, easily knocking it out of place. It floats away on the low gravity as I slam my thruster into the rock. My data pad dings as it starts analyzing the new mass and shape.

"Damn good thinking," the Captain whispers in my ear. "The computer is recalculating. We'll have your new coordinates in a few moments."

As I'm running back to Nick, my data pad dings. Everything has synched. The computer should be able to take care of the rest. Now we sit back until we get into Phaeton's upper atmosphere.

———

"I'm an embarrassment. I'd rather die in space than go back and face everyone." Nick is fidgeting with the tether that keeps him anchored on 753Qingdao, flicking the carabiner latch open and closed, threatening to set himself free.

"What the hell are you talking about?" I ask.

The Captain's voice breaks through, "Renegades sabotaged us. Found an entire case of wonky thrusters. You're lucky, Nick."

"See," I'm moving towards him with a large carabiner in my hand, ready to clip him to me. "It had nothing to do with you."

My datapad beeps.

The other riders are nearing the second moon. Some of the asteroids are already in place and it resembles a clay ball with chunks missing. I count fifteen riders free-floating through space, waiting for collection. It's our turn. I hit the thrusters. Our tethered asteroids pick up speed and easily enter Phaeton's upper atmosphere. The space is big enough, I could manually burst the thrusters as needed to park this sucker but I don't need to. The magnet engages, the force pulling the asteroids. Rock crunches and crumbles as our puzzle piece fits into place.

I slam the carabiner onto a free clip on Nick's suit, wrap my arm around his waist and slap our suit thrusters, sending us out of the upper atmosphere of Phaeton and back into space.

Nick struggles, his hands grip my wrists.

"Don't be a fool!" I yell at him.

Nick pauses. "You were always so much better."

"This is not a competition. We're in this together. Building moons together. Everyone counts."

"Been following your tail since college, hoping you'd notice me instead of him. Nick motions to the direction of Jack's rock. You saw him but you never saw me. You never saw me, Natalie." Nick is looking at me with puppy dog eyes.

"I've always seen you. I'm staring at you now. What are you even talking about?" I think he must be sick, some kind of poisoning or space madness.

"There's so much you don't know." He shoves me, as hard as one could shove in space, but I only drift as far as the carabiner will let me before we snap back together.

"I'm working with the Russians." I read his lips before I hear his voice in my helmet. "There are people who don't think women belong in space. They don't think we should be playing God and creating planets and moons, but more than that they want the women on terra, where they belong. And they promised me a heck of a lot more than a lifetime of vodka."

"Then why didn't *your* thrusters work?"

"That's the tricky part. A girl like Amber is easy to forget. But you. A woman like *Natalie*, with a fresh broken heart, waiting for the boy next door to scoop her up and make it all better. The offer was a dream come true. But I couldn't let them hurt you. I'd never hurt you. Never break your heart like Jack did."

What was he hoping for?

While he's staring into my disbelieving eyes, I unlatch the carabiner. I rotate my body and kick off his chest with both feet. We soar away from each other.

"Captain, did you hear that?" I ask.

"Certainly did. Leave him for pick up," the Captain orders. "We'll send help."

I hit my thrusters full force, propelling myself away from Nick.

I wonder if he was even sick during that first mission? And all this time I've been avoiding seafood. What a waste.

The feed in my helmet crackles. "Close the line to Third Officer Nick." He's moving his lips, but I don't care to hear what he's saying.

I tap my thruster again, moving further and further away from the other riders. I'm close to the edge of the galaxy out here. I could just keep going, see where it takes me. The one with the hazy lavender clouds looks nice. Maybe they have no varying shades of skin color in that galaxy, no gender, no religion, no warring countries, no evilness, no death or destruction, no lies.

The next galaxy over could be so much *better*.

"Natalie!" Jack's voice breaks through the crackling of my comm, panic in his voice.

"I'm here." I tap my thruster one more time.

I could not be here in a moment. Space could tug me away, suck me into its vacuum and spit me out somewhere else.

The next galaxy over could worship me like a God.

My heart beats in a chest that feels hollow. It's a feeling I've suffered before, a trust that's been broken, a numb disbelief, and the worst of them all: betrayal.

"Natalie!" A rider is coming at me full blast, thrusters skipping as they run out of gas. "Nat, stop!"

The next galaxy over wouldn't break my heart.

"Stop!" Jack yells.

My finger hovers over the thruster button.

The next galaxy over—

Jack slams into me, the force sending us tumbling. He wraps his arms and legs around my body before tapping a thruster to still us.

"I'm sorry. God, Nat, I'm so sorry. I came as fast as I could. As soon as Captain told me about Nick. What the hell are you doing all the way out here?" His eyes flick from side to side as he looks around.

There is nothing. We are so far from the other riders that the ship will have to collect us last.

"I was so afraid I'd lose you." Jack's eyes are intense. "I was so afraid I'd never be able to tell you…" He pauses to shake his head. "I meant what I said." He shakes me, but it's a strange motion in the hard vacuum of space. "I love you."

Betrayal burns like a fiery knife. It overshadows everything. But loss is a rapidly deflating balloon that makes my heartbeat skip painfully. I can't keep both of these emotions and him. Something has got to give.

The next galaxy over could be exempt from these warring feelings.

"I had a lot of time to think while I was riding the asteroid. We don't have to go back to Earth. We can do whatever you want. And I'm sorry I was acting like a fool earlier, but I needed you to see me through your anger."

His helmet is pressed against mine. I've known Jack for years and he's never held me this tight before. I guess that's what fear does to a person; makes you grip onto everything you're afraid of losing.

"Say something, Nat." He's got one hand around my back, the other touching the facemask of my helmet. I can see my reflection in his helmet, pale and wide-eyed.

It could take hours for recovery with nothing but the space and the stars and Jack.

The next galaxy over wouldn't have Jack.

What is it about us? We can make moons but we're still killing each other, still breaking the hearts of the ones we love the most. The ones we *should* love the most. A giant leap for mankind and two steps backwards. We always seem to do that to ourselves.

I never met the President of the International Space Committee.

I clip the carabiner onto Jack's suit. I can still love him in spite of his unlovable pieces, if he can do the same for me. I can't guarantee the next galaxy over can do the same.

Heartbeat

"Lookin' to trade, kid?" The shopkeeper's face is scarred; smudges of dirt cross his forehead, a hand-rolled cigarette bounces on his bottom lip with each word.

"You got any oil?"

He reaches under the counter and sets a tiny jar filled with amber liquid on the scarred slab of wood.

"No." I shake my head. "Motor oil."

The tiny jar disappears; a new jar with coffee colored liquid takes its place. "What else?"

"Two bolts."

One thin brow rises in interest. "Bolts? Metal like that's hard to come by." He drops an elbow on the counter, rests his chin in hand, taps stained fingertips on a hallowed cheek. "What's a kid like you wantin' bolts for?"

Ash drops from the cigarette in a flutter of flakes like snow from old picture books.

"Wheelbarrow needs fixing."

"Hm." The shopkeeper reaches behind the counter again. "Still using wheelbarrows these days?"

"Still buying potatoes from the commune down the road?"

Shopkeeper grunts as he pushes himself to standing using the counter as support. "Work there?"

"Work lotsa places."

"Best potatoes for miles." The shopkeeper drops two bolts next to the jar of oil. "Soil's so rotten nothing else will grow." He pinches the cigarette between his fingers, sets it on a rusty can filled with ash and tiny bits of rolling paper. "Last two bolts for fifty miles, at least. Been keeping them underground. Ever had a tomato, kid?"

"What's a tomato?"

The shopkeeper laughs, hearty and deep until he starts coughing uncontrollably.

I wait for him to calm down, itching to get out of this place. Don't like the dim of the shops. Don't like the closeness, lack of safe places to hide.

"Tomato was a—" The shopkeeper glances behind me. "Don't worry about it. Plenty of things from the oldworld you'll never taste." He sets his hand over the jar and the bolts. "What's your trade?"

Reaching into my pack, I pull out a coyote hide and set it on the counter.

This elicits a double eyebrow rise from the shopkeeper. He spreads both of his hands across the gray fur, petting it.

"Used to have a German Shepherd, 'fore the world went to shit." Shopkeeper clears his throat. "Had him at my side for a long time. Since I was a kid. Dusters came in one day, took him away," he knocks on his pant leg, a hollow sound, "took 'em both. Dog and leg. Ate 'em for dinner no doubt."

"That was nobody's pet. Caught it in the wild."

"Worth more than a baby food jar of oil and two bolts." The shopkeeper picks up his cigarette, takes a deep drag, exhales the smoke from his nose.

"I can catch a live one for you."

Dark eyes focus on me. "Shouldn't make promises you can't keep."

Stretching up on my toes, I pluck the cigarette from his mouth, take a deep drag, exhale the smoke in a staccato of rings.

"Once upon a time it was illegal for a kid your age to smoke."

"I keep my promises." I nod to the pelt, exhale a last mouthful of smoke. "Favor equals a favor."

"What do you want?"

"Need five by seven sheet of stainless steel, two more bolts, three nuts."

The shopkeeper whistles. "That kind of metal will get your ass added to the registry. Before you know it, kid, authorities will be hauling your scrawny butt off to the smelter."

The shop windows darken; didn't think the sepia haze of the world outside could get any darker.

"Probably them now." The shopkeeper grabs the pelt.

I grab the oil and bolts, shove them in the hidden pocket of my pack.

"The metal?" I ask.

"The dog?"

After a quick calculation, "Two days. Maybe less."

The flooring rumbles under my feet.

"Guess we meet again in two days." The shopkeeper drops to his knees, pulls open a trapdoor and climbs inside.

I adjust my pack and run out of the shop.

The world outside is a windstorm of dust. A Sentinel hovers over the building that houses the shops, no doubt scanning the inhabitants. Sprinting for the edge of its shadow, I'm eager to escape them finding what's hiding in my pack, eager to escape the pulse of the drone scanner increasing its radius.

Boom.

Ten feet.

Boom.

Twenty feet.

Boom.

I leap to the edge of the Sentinel's shadow, claw at the air, hit the dirt knees first and roll.

Boom.

Clear.

I scramble to my feet, add more dust to the drone wind and take off for the mountains in the distance. The bolts start to clang against the glass of oil. Afraid of it breaking, I swing the pack to my front and hold it against my chest. Precious cargo. Took me months of scouting out that shop to work up the courage and ask for what I really wanted. Took me months of hiding in the shadows, figuring out how to dress, swear and smoke. A mountain education didn't teach me any of that.

I run through narrow streets, foul smelling and dark, until I reach the dirt road that leads to the mountain.

This land used to be rich. Grass covered every inch, there was a river, trees. Now it's all ocher and dryness. Few live very far from the shops, the pipes that trickle rust stained water and government slop for dinner.

As far as I know I'm the farthest away with an eight mile hike to the base of the mountain. I rarely ever walk the full eight miles though. I've got underground tunnels that get me where I need to be.

"Jessie?"

I stop in my tracks at the sound of Nettie's voice. Should have known better, I'm never able to get past the barn without her noticing.

The old woman moves from behind a potato stand built into the front porch of her house. Rotting rattan bins are nearly empty. "What are you running from?" she asks.

Shifting my pack into place, I catch my breath. "Drone at the shops."

"No reason to run unless you're hiding something." Nettie settles her fists on her hips. "You're not hiding something. Are you?"

"Course not." I pat my bag. "Just had to pick up a few things." I point at the mountain. "They want me back before dark."

"Was a time when sending a kid your age out to traipse across burnt-up land like this was illegal." Nettie rounds the potato stand. "Your people have more stock for me?"

"Just brought a batch three days ago."

"Know how folks are nowadays. Food like that, few and far between. Sold the potatoes for a price. Kept the crew here turning new soil to get our crops up and running again." Nettie's eyes narrow on my pack. "I'd like to purchase more stock."

I take a step back. "I'll tell them."

Nettie cocks her head to the side. "Heard a rumor your people like to fix things."

My heart thumps. *My people.*

Nettie walks to the potato stand, reaches to the shelves behind. She's carrying a figurine as she walks towards me. Holds it out. "Can they make it dance again?"

I've never seen anything like it before. A human figure, thin arms and legs, erected on the point of a tiny foot, slender fingers reaching for the sky with the strangest clothing—muted pink, frilly cloth around its waist.

"Ballerina. Someone gave that to me a long time ago." Nettie holds the figurine at the base. "Innards are plastic." She flips it over, presses a button on it's back that pops open a door. "Started using plastic when the great metal harvest began."

The mechanics are transparent, the tooth of a gear is broken, jamming the motor and a spring is bent to the side.

"Means a lot to me." She snaps the door closed. "Think your people could fix it?"

"Most likely." I reach out to take the figurine.

Nettie steps close. Too close. "Better bring this back now. Don't care how many bushels of potatoes you bring. This here's special to me." She pushes the figurine against my hand. "If you don't bring it back—"

"I'll bring it back." I shove the thing in my pack.

"Why they always sending you out to run their errands?" Nettie glances at the mountain.

"I'm the fastest."

Nettie doesn't seem impressed. Her thin lips press in a straight line. "Better be on your way."

With a quick nod, I head for home.

Nettie isn't so bad. The woman could be sweet, could be a viper if need be. I don't think she ever had kids; maybe that's why she takes such an interest in me. Some women are like that; nurturing, protective of the feral children they find. At least, that's how they are in the books.

This last stretch of land is the worst. There's no shade on the road and the sun is nothing more than a punishment in the sky.

There's one more house I have to pass. The man who lives there likes to be called Mister.

"Hey kid."

I startle, didn't notice him hiding in the shadows beneath a cluster of craggy leafless trees.

"Mister." I keep walking.

"Where you headed so fast?"

Slipping my left hand into my pocket, I grasp the bone-knife hidden there. "Home."

"Strange. You call that mountain home. Was up there yesterday, didn't see a single trail, house, or garden."

"Must not've looked hard enough."

Mister pushes away from the tree, takes a step in my direction. He's tall, feet taller than me. He's younger than Nettie and the shopkeeper. There's something about Mister that makes the hair on the back of my neck stand at attention. He's a bad man.

"Was a time a kid your age was sold for a pretty penny, or a cup of coffee, warm bed." He glances at the mountain. "Could sell you for more than a pile of scrap-metal."

I take two steps away. "That mountain would hunt you down. They'd never let you do that to me."

Mister looks me up and down, head to toe. "They'll probably sell you themselves when the time comes. When you're ripe."

"No." I start walking, don't want him to see me run, don't want him to see that he scares the shit out of me.

Mister laughs, doesn't stop until I can barely hear him shouting, "Everyone does it. Can't buy innocence like you anymore."

Screw this.

I run.

I run until the meeting with Mister is nothing more that a memory, until the only thing I feel is excitement from the approaching comforts of the mountain.

There's a howling in the distance, the sound of a pack on the run, searching. Searching just as desperately as the rest of us.

The land here's so flat Sentinels are visible from a hundred miles away. At night they're difficult to see but I notice the silent flicker of a red beacon in the distance.

I need to get underground.

Dropping to my knees near a slowly dying Joshua tree, I dig with my hands. Heavy sand slides through my fingers, blows into my mouth and eyes with the evening wind. I feel the sharp pang of a busted fingernail. Sliding my hands along the wood, I grip the handle and pull, slip below ground. The night wind will cover my tracks and the trapdoor access.

This space is left over from the old government. Prewar. That's what the manuals say. Reinforced with feet of concrete, a hundred drones could be above scanning and never know what's hidden under this mountain. Room upon room, supplies, electronics, water recycler, clothing stranger looking than the dim rags worn by the people down at the shops, a thousand feet of impeccably labeled bins with freeze dried foods, foods I've never seen or heard of besides on the smooth pages of the *Encyclopedia Britannica* from the library. Under the mountain, there's everything a small group of people would ever need to survive a hundred years or more. If they didn't mind living in the past.

The computerized imitation of a barking dog greets me. Gears hum, nearly-bare rubber tires slip on smooth concrete floor.

"Hi, Samson." I pat the mechanical dog on its head.

Dim lights illuminate the hall. The generator running on min-power for years provides just enough light.

Beep. Bop. Samson follows me, his wheels squealing.

I set my pack on a chair and dig through it. I pull out the jar, bolts, and the figurine that Nettie wants my people to fix. I set everything on the workbench. Oil sloshes in the jar. I open a drawer, pull out a brush, dip it in the oil then paint it on Samson's squeaky parts.

I never caught that wolf. I didn't skin it or stretch it. I pulled it off the wall of one of the rooms below the mountain. There are other animal hides in there; exotic cats, rhinoceroses with the horns intact, otter, beaver and more. Recollections of what once was wild, someone thought important to preserve. Never liked that room much. Understand the idea of hunting; there is just something creepy about filling the room with dead things.

This will be the third time I've been in the room.

I flip on the light. Samson is at my heels, the only sound he makes come from his nearly bare tires. A wolf hide is attached to the same wall as the coyote, creatures that are a mix of man's best friend and fearless hunters. I pull the hide off of the wall and run out of the room. It feels haunted in there.

The wolves live on the other side of the mountain. Away from the shops and the farm and the creepy man. The wilderness side. Creatures roam free, predators that would eat their young before starving to death. The wilderness looks different; the sky is bluer, there's grass, dust doesn't choke the air. The humans never cross the mountain, we're not allowed.

The wild side of the mountain still has a river, the banks thick with mud. I wait until dusk, take off all of my clothes and roll in the mud until it's generous on my skin. I drape the wolf pelt over my head and down my back, pray that the wildlife over here doesn't recognize me for what I really am.

At the base of the mountain is a small cave. The alpha roams not far from the opening, head down, eyes sharp. He lifts his snout to the rising moon and releases a thrilling howl. The pack takes off.

I make my move.

The cave is dark, moonlight reflects off of ten sets of eyes. They near the opening to the cave, interested in this mud caked animal. Pot-bellied and long legged, the pups amble closer. A frail squeak echoes. Out wanders the runt of the litter, half the size of the others. I don't hesitate before reaching in and grabbing the pup. I hold it close to my chest and take off running for the mountain.

The wolf pup is warm, a tiny fire in my hands. I get home and cleaned. Samson has never worked harder in his robotic life. The wolf pup litters the floor, tears the corners off of carpets and blankets. All of that is forgotten when it crawls into my bed at night, curls up next to my side. I've never been so warm in my life. Never had a pet with a heartbeat.

I hand Nettie a bag of potatoes. Behind the barn, off in the distance, drones are digging up the land, dredging something rusted and creaking out of the ground.

"They been working on that for two days. So heavy drones keep bustin' their own parts."

"What is it?"

"Old tractor. Must've gotten stuck in the mud eons ago." Nettie uses her hand to shield the sun. "Slated for the smelter. Tragic really. If someone could get it running, would help turn the soil faster than them." Nettie thumbs towards one of the fields. Two women and three men are digging.

A whining sound breaks the moment of silence.

Nettie's eyes zero in. "What've you got there?"

I press my hands against the pack, soothing what's inside.

"Don't hold out on me, Jessie. Your people dealing livestock now?"

"No." I back away.

Nettie frowns, disbelieving. "Did they fix my ballerina?"

"Nearly. Just a few more days. I'll bring it as soon as it's done," I promise.

Nettie lifts the bag of potatoes. It's enough to distract her from what's in my bag.

"Better be on your way, kid."

I turn and head for the shops.

The door groans, wood on wood hinges that swelled with the last rain season, then dried, cracked, the empty space filled with sand and lament.

"You're back." A cloud of smoke surrounds the shopkeeper.

I close the door, lock it.

"Straight to business."

"Yes."

Walking past frayed clothing, hats that have lost their form, glass plates and ceramic teacups, I stop. The teacups are like nothing I've seen before. The mountain doesn't have teacups like this—solid porcelain, chipped, filled with shiny glue. Cups that echo of life. I select a pale blue one, start walking again. I make it to the wooden countertop, set the teacup down, adjust my pack.

"Did you get what I asked for?"

The shopkeeper crouches behind the counter. When he stands again he places the pieces of metal that I requested in front of me.

"I'd like to add the cup."

"Bring what I asked?" He sets his cigarette in the can of ash.

I swing my pack to the front, unzip it, use two hands to pull out the wolf pup.

The shopkeeper barely moves.

"That's not a German Shepard."

"Don't make German Shepards anymore." I set the pup on the counter. "At least not in these parts."

Sharp nails scrabble until the pup gets a grip in the deep scars of the countertop.

The shopkeeper looks indecisive. He eyes the pup.

"What if that thing eats my face in the night?"

"Better one night with a friend than a lifetime alone." Picking up the cigarette, I take a drag.

The wolf pup whines. I set my free hand on the back of its neck, feel the warmth, the softness of its fur, the bones of a spine that tell me all I need to know about how the pack treated the runt of the litter. It stops whining, settles on its belly, rests its chin on the counter.

I take another drag of the cigarette. Let whatever the shopkeeper rolled up in there give me strength.

"The cup will cost you."

I jam the cigarette into the can of ash, unzip my pack and pull out a box, slide it across the counter.

"What's in that?" he asks.

"Open it."

Stained fingers, nails blackened and skin scarred, the shopkeeper rips the top of the box off. "Sweet lord." He pinches the stem between two fingers, lifts. "Where did you get this?"

"The mountain."

While he's distracted, I grab the metal and the teacup, shove it in my bag and back away.

"Last time I tasted one of these… was younger than you." He glances up, doesn't seem to care that I've made it halfway to the door.

The shopkeeper lifts the fruit to his nose, closes his eyes and inhales. The pup stands, sniffs at his arm.

My back is against the door.

The shopkeeper licks the fruit, settles his lips against it and sucks. Seems he's unsure of what to do. The fruit couldn't last more that a bite, or a mouthful. The label said *Roma*, took less than a heartbeat to rehydrate.

I run out of the shop with my bounty. Drones are off in the distance, headed this way. I run past Nettie's potato stand. I run past Mister's creepy shadows. Don't have time to stop and chat. Need to get this stash underground.

Sentinels are getting closer, faster. It's like they *know* I've got a pack full of metal. They want it.

Behind an outcropping of rocks, I drop to my knees at the Joshua tree, dig and dig and dig.

The earth dances under the pulse of the Sentinel scanners.

Boom.

Fifty feet.

Boom.

Forty feet.

Boom.

Pull the trap door, slide and scramble.

Boom. Boom. Boom.

The drone's scanner picked up the hint of metal. Now it wants in.

Rocks and dust fill the narrow hole. I slide, spin, push off with my heels to go faster. Pebbles slide down with me. Cool air hits my back. The change in angle, a flat floor. I'm going too fast to stop. Head over heels, pebbles blast my face, the sheet of stainless stabs me in the side as I roll. The drone is still trying to pound its way in. I scramble to my feet, hear the familiar sound of Samson in the hall on his way to greet me.

"Go to sleep," I shout to the robotic dog.

Silence.

I slap the red button near the door. The mountain pulses, a slab of iron slams down to block the tunnel. I am tossed to the side as the mountain blows the access tunnel.

There goes my fastest route to town.

Drones will be digging for days, won't find a thing but rock before they give up. They won't dig deep enough to find the blocked access.

I roll, limp to my feet, find Samson in the dim illumination.

"Wake up." The dog comes to life, barks, wheels around me. "Good boy."

Warmth oozes down my side. I shrug off my pack. The stainless steel edge ripped through the burlap and stabbed me in the ribs. I can sew the pack. I lift my shirt, skin flaps with the movement revealing a gaping hole. Guess I could stitch up myself as well.

Samson's head tics to the side, he whines.

"I'm fine."

I empty the bag.

The teacup shattered. Nothing but chips and shards of porcelain. That's disappointing. I planned on imitating a picture from a book, drinking tea with my pinkie-finger extended *just-so*.

"Get the med kit."

Samson goes, squeaking away down a dark hallway.

I peel off my shirt, walk to the kitchen and clean the wound. A mountain education got me a few things, including basic medical training. I drop the shirt on the floor. Samson returns, spitting a med kit at my feet. He collects the torn shirt and takes it away. I'm not sure where he takes it. I just know it will be returned, cleaned and folded. I don't know everything about the mountain and how it works. Ginger went dark before I learned those details.

After dousing my wound with antibiotic powder, I think better of the stitches and decide on a pressure dressing.

I get a fresh shirt, return to the workbench and get to work, fixing Ginger.

Ginger is a leftover from early twenty-first century engineers, prewar, of course. Buried in the mountain by the people before, to help. Buried with a mountain full of junk, enough food to last a lifetime and… me.

Blue lights and decorative paint give Ginger a human-like appearance. Loose in the joints, a bit shabby, scraped and marred. He is not human, earned his name from the bright orange paint job, but he's real to me.

Samson got in the way, Ginger tipped over and smashed his case. There isn't too much broken inside, just the bolts that held certain things in place.

I reach for my tools, scoot closer in my chair. Holding a flashlight in my mouth, I grip the bolt and twist the nut securing the projector in place until it's tight. Something's not right, too much tension on the other side of the support. Another bolt head snaps. Rust clouds the air as the bolt head bounces off of the inner chest plate, ricochets, hits me just below the eye.

I mutter words learned at the shops, throw the wrench across the room.

Samson spins after the tool, sweeps it up in his collection chamber and returns, spitting it out at my feet.

I need more metal.

The fixed ballerina figurine smiles at me from the corner of my worktable. I shove it in my bag.

I leave in the dark, watch the drones as they try to tear the farm equipment from the poisoned land. Creaking, screeching of metal on metal pierces the night. The arm of a drone snaps off.

I make a run for it.

The busted drone flies away, its replacement a red beacon in the distance. I've got five minutes before the next one shows up.

The drone arm broke on a joint, twisted metal reveals innards of tiny bolts, springs, everything a kid like me could ever want. I drag the arm, settle it between my legs and start working, disassembling everything I can get my hands on. Ragged edges rip my skin, blood streaks steel. I get five bolts, four springs, a handful of bushings, a few gears, six nuts, two bloodied fingertips. I shove the collection in my pocket.

Boom.

Dust kicks up under the flight path of the oncoming Sentinel. I stand, run. Round the barn, drop down next to the potato stand.

Nettie's front door opens, she's standing there in bedclothes, a bone sword gripped in her hand.

"Jessie?" She sets the weapon down. "What are you doing out here at night?"

I open my pack, pull out the figurine and pass it to her. "Had to deliver this."

I flip the switch. The ballerina twirls on dainty toes.

Nettie's expression softens. "There was a time…" She clutches her free hand to her chest. In the moonlight, her eyes turn glossy. "You shouldn't be out after curfew. Can't believe your people would allow it. If the Sentinels hear you—"

"I'm quiet."

The twisting screech of metal on metal echoes.

Nettie leans, gets a glance at the drone working in her backyard. "Won't be sleep again tonight. You better go, while it's distracted."

I take off, running under the terracotta moonlight that's so different from the pale silver described in the books. Plenty is different now; the light, the creatures, the people. It's like the author who wrote those books in the mountain came from a different planet. It's like—

Hands grab me. I stumble, nearly fall before being lifted.

"Hey, kid," Mister's voice is nothing but sinister. His eyes are dark voids.

My heart thumps against my chest.

The ground rumbles as the drone works two miles down the road.

"Went back up on that mountain. Nothing's there." Mister grabs the back of my jacket. "You know what I think, kid?"

I struggle to break free. "Don't care."

"I think you been lying all this time about your *people*." Mister drags me against his body. "Told you, I'll get a pretty penny for you." He licks my cheek.

"Get away from me." I try to kick but he steps on my feet.

Mister's hand tugs my shirt up. "Nothing can save you out here. Not even your people. Not even whoever you're actually living with up there on that mountain."

Never had a reason to scream before, but this seems like a good time. The perfect time to test my vocal chords. I scream, louder than I've ever screamed in my entire life.

Dust blows as Mister slaps his hand over my mouth. He backs me against a dying tree trunk. Craggy bark digs into my skin, snares my hair in its grooves.

The replacement drone's red beacon shifts in the sky. The pulse on this Sentinel is softer, the searching throb barely vibrates the ground.

Mister is saying things, terrible things a kid my age should never hear. He's so busy trying to figure out the ties on my pants he doesn't notice the wind has shifted.

Boom.

Mister tugs at my clothes.

Boom.

I reach in my pocket.

Boom.

"Gonna make your people wish they never let you outta their sight." He licks his lips.

Boom.

I shove a handful of screws and bushings in Mister's open mouth. Push my fingers across his wet tongue, deep down until he gags and swallows.

Boom.

The drone lights up green. It's found metal.

Mister's eyes go wide as the drone's arms latch onto his shoulders. Blood seeps around its pinschers.

I drop to the ground, still underneath Mister's shadow as he's lifted to the collection chamber. He's screaming now, screaming words a kid my age should never hear.

I flip him the bird, a gesture learned at the shops. I lay still as a stone while the drone takes off, returning to the smelter with its bounty.

After the dust settles, I make my way back to the mountain.

I run across open desert, three miles under the moonlight with my heart beating out of my chest, fresh tears waiting to fall. I never thought a bad thing before, but I hope the government rips Mister apart getting those bolts out of his gut.

Wolves are howling. Probably looking for their missing pup. I wonder if they programmed Samson to howl when I'm gone?

I drop down next to three boulders; they're giant, look like they rolled off the mountain. The middle one is hollow. I snap open the trapdoor and slide to safety.

I use the newly collected screws and nuts, secure the slab of stainless in place over Ginger's back. The steel doesn't match the rest of the paint job, but it'll do.

Samson makes a panting sound, nudges my foot.

"I know. I know." I pat Samson on his head. "Been a long time."

I push the red button.

Ginger hums to life. Chirps and beeps as he runs through the startup program.

Eyes blink. "Hello. Jessie."

Samson's tires slip and slide as he spins in circles with animated excitement.

"You're back."

"How long has passed?"

"Fourteen months. I want to see him."

Ginger raises rudimentary arms, tests his grips, gyrometrics beneath skirted legs roll him in a circle.

The machine opens a port on its chest, video plays across the room on the flat wall.

A man in black slacks, a white dress shirt and black tie says, "Sweetheart." The voice, familiar, I've tried a hundred times to remember but never had it this perfect. "You've grown."

Everyday for thirteen years, I woke up to the same phrase.

I reply with my typical response, "Can't stop growing."

The man smiles, proud. He's just as handsome as I remember. High cheekbones, a dimple in his chin. The boys and men of the shops pale in comparison.

"I've missed you," I say. Even though he is only an image of black and white, I imagine the true color of his eyes to be blue, swirling, mesmerizing, a cloudless sky.

I might be just a kid but I'm old enough to know that the man on the wall is nothing more than an animation, voice recordings that've been altered, restrung into new sentences, programmed to adjust to my age and respond to certain conversations. Still, this hasn't felt like home since he's been gone.

He squints at the machine projecting his image; squats down like a street merchant inspecting a broken wheel. "How did you fix it?"

"I left to search for parts."

"It's not safe for you to leave the mountain."

"I know. But I had to do something. I had to fix you." I step closer to the image. "The people out there aren't like the books we've read."

"They never are. This world isn't for people who break easily or must be carefully kept. Never was."

"You should have warned me."

The man blinks. Must not have a proper response programmed.

"Anyways. I did it. I fixed you."

He frowns. "You were never meant to leave. Not until the time was right."

"I got out and I got back in. But there were things I saw, things I've done."

The man in the image, his eyes narrow. "What did you do?"

I demonstrate the gesture reserved for Mister, when the Sentinel was taking him away.

"Ah, Jessie, I raised you better than that."

He did, raise me better than that, manners and all from the oldworld. Never had another soul to practice them on. When I left the mountain it seems the people out there wouldn't know a manner if it slapped them.

The image flashes and he's suddenly sitting in a high-backed leather chair. "You're of age now," he says. "You're old enough. You're people picked a timeframe."

Strange, all I've known is Samson, Ginger, and him. They are my people. I don't know the people he is talking about. Don't remember them.

His face is placid, a lake before a storm.

"But—I lost fourteen months with you."

"And you already went outside. You already saw. Now our time is done. The programming stops here."

"But, I want more time with you. I worked so hard for more time!"

He is not real, I know this, but he is real to me—all I've ever known. He is all that matters. I want to say other things, things like *you're all I have, don't leave me,* and *I—I love you.*

"We can never go back. We have right now, though." A pipe appears in his hand, and he puffs staccato rings of smoke that rise and disappear before reaching the border of the projection.

Better one night with a friend than a lifetime alone, my own words. My heart pounds in my chest. Aching, breaking. I want to throw something at him. Slap the stone that is nothing more than a projector screen at this moment. Wouldn't be as satisfying as slapping human skin. He doesn't have human skin.

"It's too late, sweetheart." He sips from a tumbler with dark liquid.

"Why?"

There is only silence as he puffs on his pipe, watching me.

My eyes burn. "Will you tell me about the world, at least? Teach me about the things I don't know?"

"I can only tell you about the oldworld. The world from the books."

The oldworld can't help me. The oldworld can't fix this part of me. This part is broken. More than just nuts and bolts and springs.

I grab a screwdriver from my toolbox and pop the stainless off of Ginger's back, twist a bolt and shut down power to the projector. The image of the handsome man on the wall fades until there's nothing but gray stone.

Collector of Space Junk
and Rebellious Dreams

(Ten years after the Venom War)

"I'm not going." Jack shoved a rolled-up map into his backpack, next to folders of half-finished homework.

"You have to go," his grandmother warned as she clucked her tongue. "Just like you have to go to school. You don't get to decide these things."

There was plenty Jack didn't get to decide. His mother didn't ask him about moving from

Sacramento to the crappy little town of Fort Bidwell, up in the mountains near the Oregon border. She didn't ask him which room he wanted in the old two-story farmhouse she'd bought. She didn't ask him what he thought about Mitchell before she'd introduced Jack to the guy. And, months down the road, she definitely didn't ask Jack about the wedding.

Jack pulled his backpack on as he muttered to himself, "Dad would kill Mitchell."

"What's that?" his grandmother turned from the stove.

"Nothing."

She emptied a pan of scrambled eggs onto his plate. "Take that off and eat." She set the pan in the sink and rounded the table to take his backpack off. "You can't go to school hungry. Do you want juice or milk?"

"Milk," Jack decided as he dropped into his chair.

He was hungry and tired. He'd stayed up way too late tracking falling space junk and plotting the drop zones on the map in his bag. He'd charged his camera and a hand-held metal detector, and tucked them away for the day, hidden in his rolled-up gym clothes.

His grandmother filled a glass with milk. She set the milk in front of him then went on to butter two pieces of toast that had popped up from the toaster, talking while she did. "Did you finish your homework?"

"Yes," he lied from around a mouthful.

She paused before buttering another piece. "She'll find out, you know. She always does. The detention notices go straight to her datapad."

Jack was silent as he ate. He thought about hacking into the school's computer system and stopping the notices from sending, but he'd already gotten in trouble for that.

"It will ruin her day." She set the toast down in front of him. "She's picking out a dress, remember?"

Jack finished his breakfast without participating more in the conversation. His grandmother went on and on about which stores she was shopping at and details of the wedding that he didn't give a damn about. He stood and she had the table cleared before his backpack was on again.

"She might not be home for dinner." His grandmother opened the back door and walked through with him. "You'll have to put yourself to bed. I'll leave a plate in the fridge."

Jack headed for the garage to retrieve his motorbike. His grandmother let him ride it to school, his mother never did. Iceman had given him the bike for his birthday. It was the latest model hover technology, not usually reserved for citizens. But Iceman broke the rules for Jack, no matter how much his mother protested. The bike was perfect for the sandy foothills and deserts and pine forests. Jack had even raced a car one time, nearly gotten to thirty miles an hour. His mom would send the bike back in an instant if she knew it could go that fast.

His grandmother looked down the driveway. "Oh, you have a friend today. Again. Isn't that sweet." She turned to him and took the bike from his hands. "Maybe you should be a gentleman and walk her to school," she suggested.

Jack glared at the girl waiting at the end of the driveway. She wore ripped jeans, a vintage NASA T-shirt, and her hair in a messy ponytail.

"I'd rather not." Jack didn't want to deal with her today. He had other plans.

"But you will." His grandmother patted his shoulder. "It would make your father proud."

Jack walked down the driveway.

"Have a great day," she shouted over the hum of the garage door closing.

Jack waved his hand in the air but didn't bother to turn around. Instead, he glared at the girl. Lexa was becoming a thorn in his side. She had that hopeful look, like a puppy begging to be played with.

"Hey!" Lexa said with a smile as he walked past her.

"Busy."

Lexa skipped a few steps to keep up with him; she was a year younger but nearly as tall as he was.

"Do you like my shirt?" she asked, holding the hemline out. "My dad said he dug it out of an old locker at work. Pretty cool, huh?"

"Whatever." Jack turned onto a side street. He didn't want to admit the shirt was awesome. It was probably pre-Venom War, the bright blue ink was faded and cracked but the cotton had held up.

"Does your mom ever bring you back shirts?" Lexa asked.

His mom hadn't brought him back a shirt since he was in grade school. And definitely not since she'd started dating Mitchell.

Jack shook off the thought and turned left.

"Hey," Lexa said. "This isn't the way to school."

"I'm not going to school." He pointed. "You go that way."

"I'm going with you."

Jack stopped. "No." He thrust his pointed finger. "Go that way. To school. Go."

She crossed her arms and straightened her back. "I'm going with you."

It was getting late and he didn't want to get noticed; Jack caved. "You've got to keep up." He started walking.

Lexa skipped after him. "What do I tell my dad?"

"You don't tell your dad. You tell no one."

Jack controlled the urge to break into a sprint. He could run faster than her, he knew it, but he couldn't risk her getting lost. Of all people, not her.

They made it to the end of the side street and took a right, walked three blocks, turned left, then went straight until they made it to the edge of town. Jack led Lexa down a dirt road lined with pale-green scrub brush. The forest slowly grew up around them the further they went. They turned down a narrow, overgrown road, finally stopping at a shed with a decaying door and sagging roof.

There was a padlock on the door. Jack reached into his pocked, pulled out a key, and opened the lock.

"Whoa," Lexa's fingers brushed over the charred metal parts as they walked inside, "how long have you been collecting this junk?"

"Don't touch." Jack slapped Lexa's hand away. "I've been filling this shack since we moved here."

"You never told me." Lexa's bag dropped to the floor as she took further interest in the shed packed with screws, bolts, and twisted bits of metal. "I thought we were friends?"

"We aren't." Jack dropped his own backpack, unzipped it, and pulled out the map and metal detector. "Don't get any ideas."

Lexa was using the bottom of her shirt to wipe the sweat off her face. "Why didn't you bring your bike?"

"I was going to, but my grandma suggested I walk you to school." Jack unrolled the map and set the thin rod of the metal detector across the paper so it didn't roll up again. "I could have used it today."

"Just exactly how many days of school have you missed?"

Jeez, she was nosy. "Don't worry about it." He'd missed enough days to gain detention every day for the rest of the year.

"What's your mom going to say when she finds out about today?"

"She'll probably banish me to Venus."

Lexa's eyes went wide. "There is no more Venus."

"Exactly."

Jack focused on the map and he reviewed his route for the day. It was a five-mile hike to where he had tracked a large piece of space debris that had fallen last night on the reservation near Soldier Creek. If he got there early enough, he'd beat the other scrappers who wore government uniforms and looked real serious about their jobs. Jack was serious too. He was collecting every bit of debris, hoping to come across pieces of the *Explorer* or the *Gridley*, or a bit of Venom technology that might help him. Everyone said the Venom were gone, even his mother, but they couldn't have been entirely eradicated.

Jack emptied a few things out of his backpack so it wouldn't weigh him down, then he grabbed the map. "Let's go."

They were over halfway there, and Lexa was swinging a stick in her hand when she asked, "How much further?" for the tenth time.

Jack checked his map. "Maybe a mile more."

"Did you bring a sandwich?" Lexa asked.

"I didn't bring a sandwich for you." Jack clicked on the metal detector and handed it to Lexa. "Start scanning."

"Why do *I* have to scan?" Lexa tossed the stick, took the thin handle, and tested its weight with her left hand. "This is really cool. How did you—"

"Don't ask." Jack pulled the camera out of his bag. "You're scanning 'cause I'm recording."

Lexa waved. "Don't get my face. My dad can't know I skipped the entire day of school. He'll kill me."

Jack dug in his bag for the last time and pulled out a pair of gloves. He handed Lexa one.

"Whatever you find, don't touch it with your bare hands."

"Why not?" Lexa asked as she was taking the single glove.

"Did you not listen at all during *History of the Venom Invasion*?"

"That's not an actual class."

"No?" Jack looked surprised. "It should be."

"Maybe in college." Lexa tugged the glove onto her left hand. "You know, if you plan on attending college."

"I haven't decided yet," Jack muttered.

They walked, Jack annoyed that he had to explain himself to her.

"What do you think of the wedding?" Lexa asked.

"What wedding?" He knew what she was talking about, just didn't want to think about it at the moment, especially not with her.

The metal detector beeped as Lexa flicked it on. "You live under a rock or something?"

Living under a rock would be easier. He could definitely ignore the fact that his mother was remarrying a tool like Mitchell. "I'm just busy." If he didn't think about it, maybe it wouldn't happen.

Lexa waved the rod and started scanning the ground. "It must be nice to be so busy that you can just ignore everything."

Jack followed the conversation through the camera. A sad look came over her face when she mentioned the wedding. He wondered what she truly thought about it. He could ask her, but he didn't want to. It was bad enough that she was following him everywhere before they were officially stepbrother and stepsister. And Jack didn't want her to be one of those sisters who spilled their guts every time things got sticky. He couldn't allow it now.

Lexa did a double take when she noticed the red camera light was on. "Delete it," she warned. "Now."

Jack skipped away, still recording.

"Delete it. I swear, if you post that—" Lexa was holding the metal detector over her shoulder, threatening to beat Jack.

He'd like to have a little bit of blackmail on her, might help him in the future. But he gave in. "Fine," Jack held up his free hand in defeat. "I wasn't going to post it anyway."

"Delete it," Lexa demanded. "And show me. My father can't know I was out here."

"Giant baby," Jack muttered under his breath as he turned the camera around and deleted what he'd filmed.

The metal detector alarmed.

"We've got something!" Lexa changed her focus and skimmed the ground.

Jack checked his map. "These might be shards and dust." He slid his finger across the paper. "It should be just a little further."

The metal detector started beeping and flashing.

Not far in front of them, smoke rose out of a deep hole. Jack glanced up at the canopy of trees to see an odd shape blasted inward, through the treetops. Bare, damaged branches hung above their heads.

"Why's it still smoking?" she asked.

"Superheated during reentry. And the ground probably insulated it overnight."

Lexa stood back. "You sure?"

"Yeah." Jack turned the camera on and propped it on a nearby branch to record. "Let's do this." Jack pulled the work glove onto his right hand. "You get that side."

Jack and Lexa crouched down next to the hole in the ground.

Lexa hesitated. "I don't really want to stick my arm down there."

"Don't be such a girl." Jack bent and reached into the hole without hesitation. A faint stream of smoke billowed out around his arm. "I can't reach it." Jack moved to his stomach; his arm up to his shoulder disappeared in the hole. He groaned, wiggled his fingers, and stretched as far as he could until his fingers brushed against warm metal. "I got it." Jack stretched further.

Lexa scrambled to her knees and reached in, her shoulder knocking against Jack's. Together they gripped the tangled metal, tugging it closer and closer with the tips of their fingers until they got a good grasp. Then they pulled.

"Harder," Jack urged.

"I can't pull much harder," Lexa complained.

They tugged, knees digging into the ground and shoulders straining. No matter how hard they pulled, the object wouldn't budge.

"It's not coming out." Lexa sat up.

Jack followed, moving to his feet. "We just need a shovel. And we'll dig it out."

They brushed the dirt off their hands.

"You've got a shovel?" Lexa asked.

"I have one back at the shed." Jack shouldered his backpack. "Come on."

Lexa grabbed the metal detector and they started jogging the five miles back to the shed.

"What do you think it is?" Lexa asked, out of breath as she slowed to a walk.

Jack was a few feet ahead, moving at a determined pace. "I'm hoping it's a piece of a Swarm ship."

"You think that's still floating around in the atmosphere from that long ago?" Lexa didn't sound convinced at the possibility. "What if it's just a weather satellite?"

"The Venom—"

Lexa interrupted. "You mean Colubrids—"

"I don't care. They're still the Venom to me." Jack was losing his cool. He didn't care to explain himself, he'd had a hard enough time trying to get his mom to understand—that's why he didn't bother talking about it anymore with her. You'd think she would understand after all they'd been through. After all she'd done.

"So, the Swarm," Lexa urged him to continue.

"Forget it."

"I want to know."

Twigs snapped under their feet. A mountain breeze struggled to upend piles of decaying leaves along their path, only the tips of the leaves waving as they passed. Jack opened his mouth to say something more, then closed it and clenched his teeth. He could tell her every rotten thought he'd had about the Venom. He could tell her the things he'd planned to do to the last of their species—if he ever found them. The thoughts he harbored extended far beyond simple rebellion of his mother's wishes. Good Ol' Black Mamba wanted to move on and forget about the Venom, live in peace, finally. Jack couldn't do that, they'd taken too much from him.

Jack glanced at Lexa from the corner of his eye; she was kicking at the dirt as they walked. She had to know, she had to feel at least a speck of what he felt.

Her head turned, she caught him in a decisive moment and flashed him a crooked smile, but it was in her eyes that Jack caught a flash of darkness. It was in that moment, he knew that he wasn't completely alone. The Venom had killed her mother, after all.

Jack finally spoke again. "They killed my dad. They're going to pay. Doesn't matter if it happens after I pull a chunk of their ship out of the ground or if I find the spatter of their dead on another piece of space junk. I'm going to find the last of them."

"You can't even drive yet. What makes you think you can take on a fleet of Venom?"

"I'll figure it out."

The shed was within view. Lexa held the metal detector over her shoulder like a bat, waiting as Jack went inside. The *clang* of him rummaging echoed throughout the forest. He emerged again, carrying a rusted shovel with a wooden handle.

"Let's go dig this mother out."

"I was really hoping for a snack break." Lexa touched her stomach.

Jack reached into his pack and pulled out a sandwich, then tossed it to her. "Shove that down your gullet."

"Did your mom make this?" Lexa asked as she unwrapped the sandwich. He took a bite. "Mmm.

Oh, gosh." She took another bite. "My dad never makes sandwiches this good. Is this turkey?"

"No clue. I'm not the one eating it."

Lexa swallowed. "Oh man, it's like she seasoned it. Like Christmas dinner."

Jack watched as she devoured the sandwich and pulled a bottle of water from her own bag. At least he wouldn't have to give up his water too.

"So what do you do all day when you're skipping school—this?" Lexa asked as they walked. "You know, since you're barely ever at school. And doesn't your mom wonder why you don't have any homework?"

"I track space junk that falls from the sky. And then I go collect it." Jack wiped sweat off his forehead. "For all she knows, I'm doing homework every night in my room. She doesn't check much. She's too distracted with… stuff."

"Like the wedding?" Lexa asked.

Yeah, like the wedding and about a million other things. Skipping school barely caught her attention anymore. Jack couldn't even get a rise out of her, she just gave him that look of disappointment with every detention notice she received.

The ground vibrated under their feet.

"What was that?" Lexa asked.

Usually it took the men in uniform a few days to show up. Jack started running; he wasn't going to lose this find. Lexa followed.

They made it back to the landing site, the noise of men digging was loud and clear.

"Crap!" Jack whispered.

"We should probably get out of here," Lexa suggested.

Jack stopped walking and they hid behind a thick tree trunk.

"I can't just leave, I left my camera at the site."

"You didn't bring it with you?"

"No. What if something crawled out of that hole while we were getting the shovel?"

"What the crap? You made me stick my arm down there." She wiped the dirt off her bare arm as though it were contaminated.

"You lived."

"Barely. Suffering at school is looking better and better with every moment I spend with you," Lexa muttered.

"You wanted to come with." Jack peered out from behind the tree. They were close to the dig site and he could see the camera perched in the vee of a tree trunk.

"Just leave it. Let's get out of here," Lexa suggested. "If my dad finds out I skipped school, he's going to ground me for eternity."

"I can't leave it. Every dig from this past year is on that camera."

Lexa sighed. "You didn't back it up."

"I did. But I need to get my camera back. If they find out about all the digs and my stash back in the shed…"

"What are they going to do?" Lexa asked. "Drag you off to juvie?"

"Technically, anything that falls from the sky is property of the government. So, yeah. They might do that."

Lexa leaned against the tree. "Perfect." She sighed. "I can't handle jail. They'll eat me alive. My dad has told me enough jail stories to scare me straight for life. I've never done anything like this before."

The men continued digging the rubble out of the ground.

Jack had a determined look on his face when he turned to Lexa. "You should probably get out of here," he suggested.

"What. Why?"

"If you don't want to get caught, go."

Lexa looked nervous and Jack understood. She didn't sign up for this.

Lexa nodded in agreement. "If they arrest you, I'll visit every weekend." She grinned, then crept away, leaving Jack alone. He didn't want to drag her into this and he'd get in even deeper crap when his mother and Mitchell found out Lexa was here with him. It was better this way.

Jack crouched down and started inching his way closer to the dig site. There were four men, two digging and two more surveying the area. One guy came dangerously close to Jack's camera.

He inched closer, shot upright, and ran a short distance to hide behind another tree trunk.

"Did you hear that?" one of the guys surveying asked.

The two men stopped digging. The other guy was on the far side of the clearing.

"Hear what?" a digger asked.

The surveyor nearest Jack stepped closer and noticed the camera that was recording them. "What the heck?" He reached for it.

It was now or never. Jack wasn't going to lose that camera. He rounded the tree and ran straight for the surveyor holding the camera.

Adrenaline pumping, Jack shouted, "Nooo!"

The surveyor looked startled when Jack came hollering out from under the shade of the forest, arms pumping. Jack jumped on the guy, grabbed his wrist, and tried to tear the camera out of his hand. The surveyor was strong, probably ex-military, but that didn't scare Jack. Iceman had taught him enough hand-to-hand combat to protect himself. He punched the surveyor in the face, kicked him in the gut, and then the shin. Jack scrambled for the camera as it fell and bounced across the ground.

Someone grabbed his ankle. "What in the hell?" the guy muttered.

Jack kicked him in the face.

The man released his hold, hands going to his busted nose that was already leaking a thick stream of blood.

Jack scrambled, grabbed the camera, and shoved it into his pocket. He turned to find the other three men coming at him.

"You little shit," one of them barked.

Jack smiled. "That's my space junk."

Four to one are never good odds, but Jack didn't care.

One of the diggers reached for his shoulder.

Jack tipped out of the way and punched him in the arm.

The two other guys were grabbing.

Jack dropped to the ground and rolled out of their reach.

The guy with the busted nose jumped into the mess, his face and hands covered in blood. He grabbed Jack's shirt, his bloody fingers streaking the cloth.

"My mom's going to kill me for ruining this," Jack complained as he kicked the guy in the stomach.

The guy groaned, bent over, and spit blood on the ground.

The two diggers tried to catch Jack again.

He ran out of their reach, scanning the large hole they'd dug in the ground. Whatever was down there was big. Jack could see writing and what looked like the burned remnants of a decal. It definitely resembled a ship. It almost looked like a piece of the *Explorer*. Finally, after all this time.

Two guys were rounding the hole in front of him, the other two at his back. Jack was running out of options and he knew it. He just wanted to see the decal on the twisted metal in the ground. He didn't have his gloves on but that wasn't going to stop him. He bent his knees, getting ready to jump—

"Stop, Jack!" Strange, that voice sounded familiar.

Something sharp pinched his back. His muscles seized. Jack tried to toss himself into the hole so he could at least see what was buried there before they dragged him off, but his legs wouldn't listen to his brain. Instead, he collapsed.

The men stood over him.

Jack blinked, his vision hazy, his head pounding.

"Shit," one of the guys said while rubbing his face.

"You know who this little bastard is?" another asked.

"I do."

Static erupted from a radio. There were clicks and beeps as they took his picture and scanned him for identification.

One of the guys crouched down next to him. He felt fingers on his pulse. Then the brushing of hair off his face. "Damn," the guys said. "This is Rob Thompson's kid."

"No shit."

"Wasn't he married to that fighter pilot, Black Mamba they called her?"

"Yeah."

Jack couldn't see much but through blurry vision, but he could make out the frown and a nod.

"This is their boy."

One of the guys grunted as he lifted Jack off the ground.

"Too bad what happened to Rob. Hey, she still single?" one asked. "Back in the day she was a sweet piece of—"

"Have some respect," the guy carrying Jack scolded.

"What? The punk busted my nose. Least she could do is take me out to dinner. Her brat kid just made our day twice as long as it should be."

His head still felt fuzzy but feeling was coming back to Jack's arms. "Shut your filthy mouths," the guy carrying him said.

Jack recognized the voice. His mom had spent nearly every day over the past two weeks talking to the guy and planning their wedding. The loss of the space junk and probably the camera and the comments from the guys were enough to inspire one last punch. Jack waved his arm and shot his bruised fist into Mitchell's chin.

Mitchell dropped Jack and the impact of hitting the ground knocked him out.

Jack woke up behind bars. His body ached; the back of his head too. Jack tried to move his arm but it was handcuffed to the bed. He moved to sit up.

"Look who's awake." It was the guy with the busted nose. He had rolled up tissues stuck in his nostrils and dried blood on his chin. "Hey, Mitchell, your kid is awake."

The footsteps were loud and similar sounding to his mother's. Jack was still. His mother didn't turn the corner, though. It was just Mitchell. What a tool.

Mitchell stood outside of the holding cell and crossed his arms. He narrowed his gaze. "You think you're calm enough for me to open this door?"

Jack stared down the man. "You can do whatever you think is necessary."

Mitchell opened the cell and stepped inside. "Don't get up. I'm sure you've got a concussion."

"When is my mom getting here?" Jack clenched his fists. He knew what his mom showing up was going to be like. First he'd get hollered at, then she'd apologize and beg for forgiveness, even though he was the one who'd done something wrong.

"I didn't call your mom." Mitchell crossed the room and stood in front of Jack. He was holding Jack's camera in his hand. He tossed it down on the bed. "What were you doing out there?" Mitchell asked.

Jack pressed his lips together.

"Wreckage is property of—"

"I know," Jack grumbled.

"Then what were you doing?"

"None of your business."

Mitchell crossed his arms over his chest and paced the room as he spoke. "You know, we've been having some problems recovering fallen space rubble. Keep showing up to sites and finding nothing but footprints. Some of those pieces were big, could have been sent to the space museum or used for research. It's just strange that they keep going missing. Isn't that strange?" Mitchell was staring down Jack now.

"I wouldn't know."

"I think you do, buddy. I think you know exactly what I'm talking about."

"I'm not your buddy."

"Hm," Mitchell sighed. "Probably not. Never had a buddy punch me in the face before." He headed for the door to the cell. "Either way, sit tight." He exited the cell and slammed the door closed.

Jack scrambled to grab the camera that Mitchell had dropped on the bed. He inspected the exterior for damage. They gave him his camera back. He never expected that. Jack pressed the power button and searched the files. The videos of his digs were gone. He searched the rest of the files, the older ones, from when he was a kid. His heart was beating with anticipation, hoping they hadn't deleted everything. Yes! The pictures from his childhood were still there. Pictures of his dad, his grandparents, the visit from Iceman when everyone thought his mother was dead. At least they'd left those pictures on the camera. Maybe Mitchell wasn't so bad after all?

They left him alone for the rest of the day. The guy with the busted nose kept staring him down from outside the cell. Every now and then he'd get up and bring food back to his desk. Steaming cups of coffee, sandwiches, reheated dinner. Whatever the guy was eating smelled wonderful. Jack's stomach rumbled.

"Hungry, boy?" the guy mocked.

Jack didn't say anything. He watched the clock on the wall. Two hours passed, then four, then five. The sun would be setting soon. If he didn't make it home soon his mother would be home and start to worry. Or not. Mitchell was probably over there right now. The guy was probably schmoozing his mother, enjoying a night off without an extra kid to get in the way.

His dad might have been dead for the past ten years but she was still married and she still had Jack. He didn't want her moving on. Jack though of the Venom; if those aliens hadn't screwed up his world, none of this would be happening right now. His dad would have never died on that attack on the moon. When he got out of here, he was going to hunt down every last bit of space junk, find a piece laced with their virus, and hunt the Venom down. He was going to kill every last speck of the species until there was nothing left. He was going to—

"Jack-Jack?" a familiar voice called.

Jack looked up.

Iceman was there.

Jack's mouth dropped open but nothing came out. There was no getting out of this mess. As the door opened and Iceman walked in, Jack kept checking the hall outside of the room expecting to see his mom march in. She never came.

Iceman uncuffed him.

Jack rubbed his sore wrist.

"Mitchell called me. I got here as fast as I could. You're lucky that I was on-planet. Want to tell me what's going on?"

"No." Jack's chin quivered, his throat felt thick. He covered his face with his hands.

There was a long period of silence as Jack tried to get himself under control. Iceman sat by his side. He was there just like he was all those years ago when they thought Fishtail was dead. Always a pillar. Always someone for Jack to look up to.

Jack swallowed hard and wiped his face dry.

"I just wanted it. I was going to dig it up. They stole it from me."

"They stole a scrap of metal that fell from the sky?" Iceman's voice was calm. "You know it's theirs. Doesn't matter who gets there first."

"But I *need* it. I need it so much more than they do."

"What are you going to do with a stockpile of twisted metal that's burned from re-entry?"

"Revenge," Jack whispered, feeling nearly embarrassed that he'd finally revealed his plan to the man he so admired. "I'm going to make the Venom pay."

"I already made them pay." Iceman looked down at his hands. "Made them pay for the both of us. Believe me, kid. There's nothing left."

"There could be," Jack argued.

"There isn't. I guarantee you. The war is over. It's been over for years."

"There's still a chance I could make them pay for what they did to my father."

"He died living. Doing something he loved. It's not wrong to mourn him. But the Swarm… There is so much more you could be putting your mind to. Focus all this energy elsewhere." Iceman cleared his throat. "You know, sometimes I worry about how easy it is to get lost in the vastness of space, but it's just as easy to get lost with two feet on earth."

"You need anything?" Mitchell was standing in the doorway.

"No," Iceman waved. "Just a few more minutes."

Mitchell nodded before walking away and leaving them alone again. Jack was glaring at the guy and Iceman noticed.

"We served a tour together back in the day. Went to fighter pilot school together too." Iceman settled his elbows on his knees and clasped his hands together. "But I've got to tell you, Mitchell is a good guy. I introduced him to Black Mamba."

Jack held back a smile. It was the way Iceman said Black Mamba, a bit of mocking and an inside joke that Jack didn't know. It was real, though. The relationship between them was so real. Jack wondered why it couldn't just be the three of them? Iceman could leave space and settle on earth. He wouldn't take his father's place but Jack would much rather have him than some guy he didn't know.

"You know, his wife died too. The Venom killed her. The same as your dad."

Jack never knew.

Iceman reached out and squeezed Jack's shoulder. "Let's get you cleaned up."

Jack stood.

"I already called your mom," Iceman said.

"Did you tell her?" Jack asked, fearing the earth shattering scolding he was going to receive once he got home.

"Tell her what?" Iceman smiled. "That you broke an ex-fighter pilot's nose and punched her boyfriend in the face?"

They let him use their locker room to wash the dirt off his face and arms and change his shirt. Jack threw his shirt with the bloody handprint in the trash on his way out.

"Hungry?" Iceman asked.

Jack nodded.

"Great. I know this place where the girls serve burgers in miniskirts and bikini tops. Your mom would kill me if she knew I was taking you there."

Jack entered an empty house and climbed the stairs to his room. He closed the door, paced for a few minutes, and then sat down at his desk and turned the monitor on. The program he designed was still tracking space junk; it always did and always would. Something fell in Alabama, something else over Nebraska, but the mass of that debris was small, probably burned up to ash then blew away on the wind. Something was falling over Canada. Jack watched the computer map its trajectory. There was plenty of debris still orbiting the upper atmosphere, just waiting to drop from the sky. Jack leaned back in his chair and watched.

The program mapped everything; the moon, the ships that were currently orbiting, old satellites, spent rocket stages, and fragments of metal and plastic from collisions and disintegration. The tiny specks were like a thousand stars circling the earth, some traveling at nearly twenty thousand miles per hour. If he zoomed out, the junk was a halo surrounding earth, a milky-white aura, subtle and luminous. Against the wishes of Iceman, Jack gazed upon the speckled playground with rebellious dreams of defeating the Venom vivid in his mind. Jack's dreams fled far and fast, to distant galaxies and new moons that hadn't been discovered, all in search of the last remaining Venom. He'd collected these dreams since his father was killed; he remembered every single one of them, he kept them stashed in the back part of his brain for safekeeping and easy recollection. It was too hard to stop digging up the past after what the Venom had done. Jack knew Iceman would be disappointed, but he just couldn't quell the desire for revenge. Could anyone, really? But, maybe, if he tried really hard…

Iceman was right, it was quite easy to lose your way with two feet planted on the earth, gravity wasn't enough to keep you centered, to cement you to the planet and keep your dreams within the boundaries of the atmosphere. Jack needed more to keep him tethered, his mother and grandmother and Iceman weren't enough. But now there was Lexa. Maybe she was enough? Maybe that was all he needed this whole time, someone who truly understood his grief.

Jack watched the screen for hours, dozing off a few times only to wake up and study the display again. And then, around three o'clock in the morning, the program highlighted a large piece of debris was falling near the Nevada border. Jack rummaged through his desk to find a new map— they had confiscated his old one and no doubt his shed filled with things that had fallen from the sky. Jack marked the drop zone on his map, then calculated how long it would take for him to reach it. On his bike, he could make it to the fall site in just a few hours.

Jack found an old backpack in his closet. He packed the map, some money from his allowance savings, and made a mental note to grab some snacks in the morning. Then he set his alarm so he could get a few hours of rest. When the sun rose, he was going to the Nevada border and he was damn sure that he was going to beat Mitchell and his crew.

Just as he fell asleep, he heard his mother walking through the house. She was finally home, but by the time she cracked open his door to check on him, Jack had already fallen asleep.

The alarm clock buzzed in the morning. Jack moved out of bed, feeling like he'd been steamrolled. He got dressed, dressed like he normally would for school, and walked down the stairs. Jack smelled waffles and heard familiar voices as he made his way to the kitchen.

His grandmother was standing at the counter; she turned to carry a plate piled with waffles to the table. His mom was sitting at the table, and if she knew what happened yesterday, she didn't let on. Iceman was there, sipping at a mug stained with coffee. Mitchell was there too; he flashed a smile. So was Lexa, looking a bit more put together than yesterday morning. Jack figured his mother had something to do with that. Lexa was always more tidy after she saw his mother in the mornings.

Jack sat at the table, feeling uneasy. He set his backpack on the floor near his chair. All of the things he'd packed for his adventure today seemed to weigh a thousand pounds.

His mom, Mitchell, Iceman, and Lexa didn't pause their conversations as he sat and his grandmother piled a plate full of waffles. His mother flashed him a quick smile as she looked him over.

"Did you find a dress?" Jack asked as their eyes met.

His mother looked shocked. "I did. I didn't think you'd care much, but yes, I did. I'll show it to you when you get home from school, if you'd like."

He nodded. He *didn't* care about the dress, but this wedding was going to happen. There was no denying it. He was going to have to accept it no matter how much he didn't want it. Or maybe… he glanced around the table at everyone. Jack was tired of feeling like an outsider. He could try harder to forgive and forget, at least a little bit. His mother had been alone all these years, maybe a change would be good for the both of them.

Silverware clanked on plates and his grandmother fussed over everyone, making sure they had enough to eat.

"So what do you think about having a sister?" his mother asked as she motioned to Lexa.

Jack was searching for the right words. For the first time ever, he was trying not to piss everyone off.

"Oh, hey," Mitchell stood, crossed the room, and brought a package over, handing it to Jack. "I found something for you."

Jack opened the brown paper wrapping and found a vintage NASA T-shirt; similar to the one Lexa was wearing yesterday. He tried to hide his excitement. "Thanks," he said, holding in a smile as he pulled the shirt over his head. It smelled strange and was a little big.

"How'd you find that?" Iceman asked.

"They were vacuum sealed at the bottom of a locker. The others went to a museum, but I managed to talk them out of two shirts," Mitchell replied.

Lexa stood and took her plate to the sink. "We're going to be late," she warned, not looking at Jack.

They walked to the door, the adults talking a mixed conversation of wedding details and space explorations.

"Have a great day," Mitchell said as he kissed Lexa on the cheek.

Jack's mother hugged him. "You never did answer my question. What do you think about having a sister?"

Jack glanced at Lexa. "Cool. I guess."

He and Lexa started walking.

"Make sure you actually go to school today," his mother called.

"The both of you," Mitchell shouted.

"They don't need school," Iceman muttered, "they need a year of exploration in space."

The last thing Jack heard was his mother scolding Iceman for being a bad influence.

"You told them?" Jack asked. He regretted bringing Lexa with him yesterday.

She nodded. "I couldn't help it. He got my detention notice."

They walked on in silence.

"Which way?" Lexa asked as they neared the corner.

The pull to walk in the other direction, towards the shed in the woods, was strong. Jack glanced behind them and saw that the adults had returned inside. He had to try. After all, it wasn't just him any longer.

The Nevada border could wait. He knew that revenge was a childish resentment he'd likely never fulfill. He'd been searching all these years and never found any semblance of the Swarm. He wasn't going to stop, though; he could dig for space junk on the weekends, at least those sites closer to home. He'd be able to dig up a lot more stuff with an extra set of hands anyway.

Jack turned toward school. "This way."

Tick of a Clockwork Heart

Emanuel Flynn McKenzie swiped a polish-laden rag over where his father's bicep should have been. There was no muscle, there was no arm. Instead there was a mechanical prosthesis, a titanium alloy complete with gears; a mixture of steel, bronze, and copper. The arm was a masterpiece, really. Although, this was hard to observe with the amount of tarnish that the arm was currently coated with.

"Son, you shine like a thoroughbred. Put some elbow into it."

Emanuel scrubbed harder until the tarnish broke and a bright patch of bronze the size of a coin was visible.

His father had an appointment. Every month he traveled through Gravendale to the Ministry of Justice. He never told Emanuel why and the boy had learned it was better not to ask.

Emanuel wondered what it was like there. Judging from the way his father was currently scrubbing the tarnish off his bronze and steel fingertips, it must be a place outside of the Drift. Somewhere the sun might reflect off of the mechanical arm, illuminating all of its metallic glory.

"Don't forget the gears." His father stopped polishing and passed a small brush laden with polish over his shoulder.

Emanuel cringed—openly, since his father couldn't see him at the moment—and took the brush to the gears. He was careful scouring around the elbow. There was a piece of metal, reminiscent of a tendon, which was broken. The break prevented his father from using much of the arm besides the fingers.

Emanuel didn't like polishing the arm and he wished his father would hurry up already and build himself a new one, or ask the Ministry for a replacement. Maybe he was waiting to find a new strip of leather? The current piece that was secured across his chest holding the prosthesis in place was worn and tattered.

By the time they were done, the prosthesis was the brightest object in the shadowed dwelling that they called home.

"Will you take me with you this time?" Emanuel knew better than to ask but couldn't help himself.

His father's lips pressed into a firm line before he said, "No. Valentine will be here soon."

"But Valentine is—"

"Responsible enough to watch over a boy of nine years." Lucas busied himself with readying to go.

"It's just strange," Emanuel began, "that a creature of—"

There was a sudden whisper of feathers, the beat of strong wings, the brunt of a feathered body shoving open the window over the sink.

"A creature of what?" Valentine asked from the sill.

The owl gazed down the line of his curved beak. It was a proper glare of great knowledge and authority.

Emanuel's mouth snapped shut.

"You'd do right to be in bed by the time I get back," his father said as he crossed the room, opened the door, and then closed it promptly behind him.

Emanuel stood still as Valentine inspected him, his amber eyes slanted. In the tense silence, the great gray owl's head spun until he was studying a fading picture on the mantle.

"Truly tragic," Valentine muttered.

The picture on the mantle was of Estella Chadwick Dellaghy. Emanuel's mother. The boy knew who she was but had only met her for a few moments after his birth, promptly before she expired. He remembered nothing of her, only had the small picture to know what she looked like.

"Why do you cringe so when you look at the arm?" Valentine's head rotated smoothly as he glanced at the boy.

Emanuel sat in a chair. "To be metaled and cogged up, it's just wrong."

It was a child's reasoning that Valentine had been diligently trying to correct.

"And to live without. To be a portion of a whole. Or nothing at all." Valentine was watching Emanuel closely. "Would that be better?"

"I'm not sure." The boy shrugged.

"Don't shrug. It's a gesture of the common folk. A class that you are above." Valentine's head spun slowly and his eyes narrowed. "Even if this dwelling begs to differ."

Emanuel's stomach grumbled.

Valentine's eyes widened a bit. "When was the last time you ate?"

The boy half-shrugged before a look from Valentine halted the gesture. "Lunch. At school."

"Sit a spell," Valentine ordered. "I'll find you something."

Emanuel shivered, expecting the old owl to return with rabbit parts or a half-rotten mouse.

When Valentine did return he dropped a package on the polished oak dining table. The aroma was superb. Emanuel opened the bag to find a roasted chicken leg wrapped in paper and a warm dinner roll with sweet cream butter. It wasn't a large meal but it was more decadent than what he and his father usually ate for dinner. Valentine watched with his large yellow eyes while Emanuel chewed the meat down to the bone then sucked on the end for a moment, as though he might get more nourishment from it. He savored the dinner roll, leaned back in his chair and nibbled around the outside. By the time Emanuel was done eating, his eyes were heavy and the darkness outside the windows were of night instead of the Drift lurking overhead.

"Best get yourself to bed," Valentine suggested.

Emanuel lifted himself from the chair and trudged to his room.

Valentine glanced out the window as the haunted island moved closer in the sky.

Valentine collected the wrappings from the boy's dinner and flew outside to dispose of them down the street.

Lucas was too damn proud to allow Valentine to do such a thing as feed his child an upper class meal without repayment. It was nothing really, Valentine already owed the man so much after he'd saved his life and nursed him back to health when Valentine was nothing but an owlet. But he knew better than to offer more than the springs and gears and formed bits of metal that he brought every few days.

When he returned, Valentine settled on the edge of the table and glanced at the picture of Estella as the creaking sounds of Emanuel crawling into bed filled the small house.

"Truly tragic," Valentine muttered to himself, again.

When the soft noises from the bedroom ceased and Valentine was certain the boy was asleep, he began his search.

There were blueprints that Lucas had been hiding from him. The man had been going to the university at least once a week to work with an engineer, one that was paid well to keep their mouth shut. But Valentine had found out, just as he always discovered things that were meant to be kept quiet.

He searched the entire house, every drawer, every cabinet, every nook and cranny, except for the locked cupboard under the sink. Valentine tried his best but couldn't open it.

In the end, he gave up his pursuit to find the blueprints and perched next to the window.

Emanuel was indeed sleeping by the time Lucas returned. The man walked in the house, looking as though he held the weight of all of Gravendale on his shoulders. Before leaving the house the man was composed and dapper, nearly the strong Captain that Valentine was familiar with. That façade had been stripped away by the Ministry's decision.

With all that he and Lucas had done for the Ministry, what Lucas was asking for wasn't much. They'd risked their lives on multiple occasions; there were secrets that they knew, secrets that could bring down the Minister. Lucas had lost his arm defending the Gravendale ship against pirates. The memory was still fresh in Valentine's mind, even after all of these years. Lucas had taken on three of the pirates, he had knocked two of them unconscious and the battle was nearly over. Valentine himself was using his talons and beak against the pirates, but what happened when Lucas went overboard, Valentine wasn't sure. He only knew that the man hit the steam-powered propeller and it sliced his left arm clean off, chopped it to bits with no hope of reattachment. During the pirate attack no one was left to steer the ship and it crashed into a grouping of rocks jutting from the sea and sank. The moments Valentine spent circling the sea, searching for Lucas, were the most frantic of his life. The Ministry hadn't paid the man enough for what he'd done, his funds were dwindling after a mere nine years, and that was a clear indication to Valentine that they wanted him back in service.

Valentine blinked the memory away as Lucas walked through the house to look in on Emanuel. Valentine could hear the man speaking softly to the sleeping boy followed by the soft click of the bedroom door closing.

When Lucas returned to the room, Valentine asked, "What did they say?"

"They said no." Lucas clenched his fist. "They always say no. All I need is a small amount. Just a few milliliters."

Valentine shook his head. "Damn apes with your damn machines."

"You have a better solution?" Lucas had a tone that Valentine hadn't heard in years, one that would send the lesser ranks of that steam-powered Navy ship running.

Valentine ruffled his feathers in concern. "Why not try a surgeon again?" He was prying, wanted to know who Lucas was working with at the University.

"They can't do anything." Lucas waved the suggestion away.

The way Lucas refused to look at him, Valentine knew it was a lie. A surgeon who followed the rules couldn't do anything. There were plenty of academic types at the University with questionable morals.

"The alternative therapies offered in Etherglen?"

Lucas shook his head. "They can't help." He looked exhausted from his trip.

"Surely there is something that can be done, possibly with a little bit of money?" Valentine asked.

"I've used almost everything the Ministry granted me burying her," Lucas's eyes glanced to the framed picture on the mantle, "and paying off the debt of her education, paying for this damned shack of a house, and keeping the boy fed."

"Shh," Valentine scolded. "You'll wake him."

"Then there was that last batch of Black Amber and that bit of iron from the Roberts brothers."

Whoo. Valentine hopped to the arm of a chair. "It was a cost you had to incur, to ensure the cog would work."

Lucas shoved both hands through his hair that was no longer neatly styled. "With each year it will get worse. A ticking time bomb."

Valentine tipped his head. "So we resume."

"If you'll continue to help me."

"I could assist you until the end and never erase my debt, Captain—"

"Don't call me that," Lucas snapped.

"Can't hide the past. No matter how hard you try."

Lucas unstrapped his boots, removed them, and placed them neatly by the door with a heavy sigh.

"Can't change what happened on that ship," Valentine continued. "It wasn't your fault."

"This is not the time. Nor the place, the boy might wake and hear." He crossed the room before asking, "Did you find it?"

There was a long pause as Valentine studied the man before revealing a quarter-inch gear in his talons. The owl took flight and dropped the gear in Lucas's open hand before flying out the window.

Lucas opened the cupboard under the sink. He pulled out a large vat, removed the top and dropped the gear inside to soak in a vile solution, one that caused bacteria to shrivel up but kept the metal clean and gleaming.

He closed the cupboard again and secured the lock. He couldn't risk losing all of the parts that he had acquired, couldn't risk the boy finding them, couldn't risk the blueprints that were in there being found. The good doctor had warned him that what they were planning was, indeed, forbidden.

Lucas stood and manually extended the prosthetic arm, felt the *click* of the broken rod near the elbow. The arm would have cost a fortune new.

He couldn't afford to replace it and he couldn't waste time asking the Ministry for a new one. It would just have to do. Lucas removed the arm and placed it across the dining table. He stretched his back in an attempt to loosen the sore muscles that supported the prosthetic.

He took a small canister of oil off of a nearby shelf and began rotating the gears. Lucas wanted to make sure the mechanisms still moved, with the chance that he might be able to fix the broken rod and use the arm properly again—he didn't want the entire thing to freeze up. Even damaged the contraption served him well, it could hold objects and the fingers worked sufficiently. He was better off with it broken than nothing at all.

His father was already in the workshop by the time Emanuel had woken and dressed for school. The boy ate alone, left the house without a goodbye, and began the short walk to school. His father was working on a project and Emanuel saw less and less of the man in recent days.

A sparrow was hopping along the fence as Emanuel walked. "*Tshee, tshee*. Boy. Boy. I say, boy!"

"Go away." Emanuel walked faster, the Drift shifting above him and the lanterns along the street illuminated the dim.

"They say your father is a lushington." The sparrow took to the air and was flying next to Emanuel now.

"They say he's a smasher." The sparrow fluttered about his head before grabbing ahold of a few strands of hair with its beak and ripping them out of his scalp.

Another joined in, this one pecking and nipping at his shoulder and upper arms.

Emanuel had to get away from them or he'd be a bloody mess by the time he arrived at school. Last time there were three sparrows, and they left him with scratches to his face and a bloody ear. His father was called to collect him that day.

The two sparrows were flapping on each side of his head, taking turns with the insults, the scratches, and plucking hair from his scalp.

"They say he's soaked."

"They say he's a skipper."

Emanuel could feel his throat clogging up. He started to run, trying to get away from the pesky sparrows.

"They say he's a shivering jemmy."

"They say he's a snoozer."

Emanuel's heart was beating faster. His chest was starting to ache from running. One of the sparrows ripped another clump of hair from his scalp.

"*Tshee*. They say he's nickey."

"*Tshee*. That's right. They say he's half seas over."

"They say he's a deadbeat."

"They say he's a cracksman."

"*Tshee*!" The sparrow on the right shrieked.

"Stop running, boy," a familiar voice took the place of the pesky sparrows.

Emanuel came to a full stop, clutching his chest, and looked up.

Valentine was soaring, a sparrow in each talon. He shucked them high into the sky. "Skedaddle, crowbait."

Emanuel leaned against the fencing that bordered the walkway. He held his chest, the muscles tight and mostly out of breath, tears welling in the corners of his eyes. He coughed and wiped at his face, couldn't let Valentine see him crying like an infant. Valentine might tell and Emanuel knew his father would be disappointed in his weakness. Emanuel was already small for his size, exceptionally fair skinned and feeble muscled.

Whoo. Valentine landed at Emanuel's feet. "Annoying creatures those sparrows can be."

Emanuel nodded and wiped his eyes, silent.

"No point in hiding it from me. Even with the cover of the Drift these eyes see all." Valentine moved closer. "Are you well?"

Emanuel's heart had finally stopped pounding and he felt like he could breathe again. "I think." He nodded.

"Up with you then." Valentine tipped his head, motioning for the boy to stand again.

Emanuel stood and adjusted his clothing.

Valentine noticed that the boy was unusually pale after standing. Paler than he should be for running a short stint like that. Perhaps it was the aggravation of the sparrows? Or perhaps the warnings from Lucas, of what to expect, was so fully upon them that it was too late.

"Are you feeling well?" Valentine asked.

Emanuel placed his hand over his chest. "It feels like my heart is beating so fast." He coughed. "It hurts a little." The boy pointed just left of the center of his chest. "Right here."

The memories of Estella came to the forefront. Lucas had told Valentine everything, the reasoning behind her death in childbirth, the expectation that the same disease of the heart would inflict their son.

It is just a matter of time, the doctors had said, *during infancy, childhood, anytime really. The best you can do is prepare yourself.*

Valentine could remember the way Lucas repeated the physician's words, that faraway look in his eyes, the slack of his face, the crushing weight of devastation that had caused once strong shoulders to slump.

Most of the time, Valentine could barely recognize his old friend. Valentine and the Captain had participated in numerous voyages in the name of Gravendale, but the day that steam-powered Navy ship crashed forever changed his good friend's life. Valentine imagined losing a wing would impair his life as well, it was all of the other occurrences that made him wonder if someone had laid a curse to Lucas the day he married Estella.

"Sit," Valentine told the boy.

Emanuel collapsed onto the walkway. The shadows of the Drift shifted and a streetlamp flickered.

"Don't move from this spot." Against his better judgment, Valentine flew off to secure a carriage to transport the boy. There was a driver who owed him a favor, Valentine had run more than one questionable errand for the driver and now was as good of a time as any to collect.

Valentine knew the boy couldn't attend school the way he was; he also couldn't go home to worry his father. Lucas needed to finish what he was working on, there was no doubt in Valentine's mind that Lucas currently had the kitchen and the workshop covered in tiny bits of metal, gears and springs and things, and those blueprints. He'd never clear the mess before the boy saw it if they went home now. Valentine figured a day spent exploring in a carriage would raise the boy's spirits and give him time to rest and recover.

Emanuel's eyes were as large as an angler bug's when Valentine pulled up riding on top of the carriage.

"Get in, boy." Valentine flew down to nudge the boy into the back of the carriage.

"I've never ridden in one of these before." Emanuel stepped up into the carriage, waited for Valentine to enter, then closed the door.

"I've ridden in many. With your father. Before your birth, of course."

"Really?"

Emanuel looked excited and it worried Valentine, he didn't want the boy stressing himself any further today.

"Lie down and rest," Valentine instructed. "You've had a rough morning. When you wake, we'll stop for tea."

Emanuel shifted on the bench, rested his head on the plush seat, and drifted off to sleep.

As the boy slept, Valentine instructed the driver to circle the lake a few times. Valentine kept a close eye on him, relieved when the boy's paleness dissipated. He was even more relieved when the boy's eyes opened hours later and he sat up.

"I'm quite hungry," Emanuel announced.

"Very good."

The autocarriage continued on for a few more minutes before coming to a stop at a storefront.

Valentine motioned for Emanuel to get out and follow. They entered a teashop that didn't appear to be open. Shops like this, ones that were questionable and dark, were always open for Valentine.

Emanuel was quiet as he took in the shop. Valentine brought him to a table in the back.

"Sit," he told the boy. "I'll order for us."

Valentine flew to the counter to speak with the shop owner then returned to the table and perched on the corner of it.

After a few minutes a waitress brought over plates of food and teacups for the both of them.

"What is this?" Emanuel asked as he looked into the teacup of purple liquid.

"Grosse baum tea."

Valentine picked at his own meal of stewed meat while Emanuel ate the same. He tried not to think of the beating Lucas would give him if he knew he'd fed the boy the tea. Lucas could never afford the dark purple needles collected from an ancient tree in Etherglen. Most couldn't, but Valentine had debts owed to him, and Valentine owed a debt to Lucas, this was a truly gray area that tested Valentine's standards.

After eating, they returned to the carriage. It was finally late enough for Valentine to return the boy home. He instructed the driver as to where to drop them.

"You mustn't tell your father any of this," Valentine warned as Emanuel closed the door to the carriage.

"Why not?" Emanuel asked.

Valentine knew the boy was quite frightened of him and decided it was best to manipulate the child a bit than risk Lucas discovering where they had been for the day. He'd done worse, much worse, to ensure secrets were kept.

"I'll tell him that you were a bleary-eyed mess when the sparrows teased you." Valentine narrowed his yellow eyes.

The boy crossed his arms. "Fine." He settled back on the bench as the carriage took off.

The ride was tense and silent before the carriage came to a stop a few blocks from the house.

"We walk from here," Valentine said as they got out. After a few short words with the driver, the carriage pulled away.

"Found this beast lurking about the neighborhood," Valentine said when Lucas opened the front door.

Something froze up inside Emanuel recalling their deal; he couldn't even open his mouth to greet his father.

"Don't let him scare you, he's mostly feathers." Lucas patted his son's head and motioned for him to come in.

Valentine nodded and flew off without another word.

There was something shiny on the dining table. Just as the gleam of it caught Emanuel's eye, his father crossed the room with a few quick strides and threw a cloth over the thing.

"What was that?" Emanuel asked.

"Nothing, son." He moved the cloth-covered thing away. "Are you hungry?"

Emanuel wasn't necessarily hungry after the adventures of the day but he nodded his head. A meal with his father was a rare event.

His father placed a steaming cup of tea in front of him. Emanuel sipped at it while his father began cooking at the stove. This tea was much different than the tea had had drank earlier in the day, infused with chamomile and spearmint, Emanuel frequently drank this before bed to help him sleep. The tea he had earlier was refreshing, but unusual. Emanuel smoothed his had over his chest recalling the way his pain had disappeared after drinking the purple tea.

Suddenly there was a *crash* and the *ting* of a thousand metal pieces bouncing to the far corners of the small house filled the room. Emanuel looked up to see that his father's arm had fallen off, the leather strap that held it in place had finally snapped.

Emanuel moved to help pick up the pieces.

"Don't," his father snapped.

Emanuel froze. There was a tone in his father's voice that warned him not to disobey.

"Sit down. We'll eat first. Deal with that later."

His father plated the meager dinner. It took two trips to bring both plates to the table. His father sat, poked at the small meal of lamb and rice before he finally started eating.

His father looked strange without the prosthetic.

"Can we fix it?" Emanuel asked, knowing that his father was tinkering. Whatever he was working on could surely take a backseat for him to make a new arm.

"Doubtful."

"What will you do for your next trip to the Ministry?"

"I shall go with one arm." His father winked. "Perhaps they will finally take pity on me and give me what I need."

Emanuel knew that his father's prosthesis had been broken for a long time. He smiled with the thought of his father being awarded a new one.

Maybe this one will have a cloth covering so Emanuel would no longer have to help polish it each week. He smiled wider with hope.

"Beat the devil around the stump and eat your dinner, son."

Emanuel ate quickly, his mind filled with all of the adventures he and his father could go on with a fully functioning prosthesis. Maybe his father could go back to work? If he could work again, they could leave this shack of a house; maybe move to New Alderhaben or one of the skyscrapers on Lake Moor. Then Emanuel wouldn't have to listen to the sparrows or the blowhards at school.

The meager dinner filled Emanuel's belly and he found himself yawning after the last bite.

"Get to bed," his father ordered. "I'll clean up."

Emanuel stood and tiptoed over the bits of metal rod and brass pieces. He turned when he got to his bedroom door. "Father?"

"What is it?" he seemed distracted with the chaos on the floor.

"I hope they give you a new arm." Then, feeling quite proud of himself for bringing up the subject, Emanuel turned, entered his room and closed the door softly behind him. He flopped down on the bed, stomach bursting full, exhausted from the events of the day, and instantly fell asleep.

Lucas glowered at the closed door, a cracking feeling in his chest. He left the dishes on the table, bent, and began picking the pieces of his shattered prosthesis off of the floor. Lucas collected the parts in two buckets; parts that could be saved, and parts that were too damaged to salvage. He kept them, though, with the intention of melting them down in the future, if needed.

When the floor was clean, and Lucas was certain that he had found every piece of metal, he finally washed the dishes. He took his time since he no longer had the help of the prosthetic.

In the long moments that passed, he found himself reminiscing about Estella, the way she would hum while cleaning up, the way her skirts swayed, the smooth waist of her corset, the contrast of black velvet against her fair skin…

Lucas shook his head, couldn't let his mind wander back to that time. He set the dishes to dry before unlocking the cupboard under the sink and dragging out the bucket he had hidden there.

Opening the lid filled the room with vapors; Lucas cracked the window over the sink so the vile aroma wouldn't wake the boy. Then he began another type of sorting. Parts and pieces from the buckets went into the solution to be cleansed and sterilized. He scolded himself for not thinking to use the pieces from his arm before now. If he had done this months ago, he could have had what he needed done in a fraction of the time.

Emanuel's footsteps echoed on the sidewalk as he made his way to school. In just a few days his father would return to the Ministry of Justice and Emanuel prayed that they'd give him the new arm.

He was lost in thoughts and dreams before the fluttering of small wings interrupted him.

One of the sparrows was back. It pecked at the back of his neck.

Emanuel started to run.

"Your father is a coffee boiler—"

A shriek from the sparrow echoed off of the close buildings as Valentine appeared; he swooped in and grabbed the sparrow in his talons. The sparrow was sputtering, "Spending too much time with your ape child." The sparrow pecked at Valentine's legs. "You're a dishonor to your kind. They're nothing but egg eaters."

Three sparrows were flying directly towards Valentine, probably with hopes of assisting their kin.

There was a cry as Valentine tore the sparrow to pieces and flung the parts into the sky.

Emanuel slapped a hand over his mouth in shock. Having never seen an act so violent before, bile rose in the back of his throat. He didn't know what to think.

Valentine flew away without a word to Emanuel.

Lucas was staring at his boots with focus. The old pair he could easily slip on, but this pair had the shiny stiff leather that went so well with his uniform and he needed two hands to tie the laces. He had already asked the boy to help him with his belt, the buttons of his shirt, and the large brass buttons of his waistcoat.

Without being asked, Emanuel bent and started loosening the laces. Lucas pushed his feet into the stiff boots and looked away as his son tied the laces for him. The boy stood afterwards, hands on his hips proudly.

"Thank you, son," Lucas said gruffly as he patted the boy on the head.

Lucas collected a few things for his travels, during that time Valentine had arrived to watch over the boy, just like he did every week.

"Father," Emanuel said as Lucas reached for the door. "Good luck! I hope they give you a smashing new arm." The boy was smiling widely.

Lucas nodded as his eyes flicked to Valentine's. Then he walked out the door, down the rickety steps of the house and onto the sidewalk. The brisk wind made his eyes water—he hoped it was the wind. It had to be the wind.

As he walked, the commoners of Gravendale stared. They used to gawk at his prosthetic, now they gaped at the empty space where his arm should be. Lucas was lucky that the accident with the ship had only taken his arm. It could have taken his life.

He walked faster, eager to avoid the prying eyes of his neighbors. At least in the areas closer to the Ministry they would just ignore him.

Lucas thought he saw movement from a shadow and picked up his pace. He wouldn't doubt the Ministry to send assassins to keep him quiet. The Ministry had paid him off and provided him with a top of the line prosthetic to keep his mouth shut when his work was done. Lucas had kept quiet for long enough. Now that he was back, he was nothing but a glaring example of what the Ministry had tried to bury. He was equal parts feared and despised, he and Valentine both. The only difference was that the old owl seemed to make it work for him. Lucas didn't have such luck.

Lucas didn't give a damn, only wanted what he asked the Ministry for each week, just a small bit of Black Amber, that was all he needed. If they kept denying him, Lucas was going to have to take the situation into his own hands; his gut told him that he was running out of time.

He glanced at the shadows in the alley; fully realizing that couldn't adequately defend himself with one arm if assassins were truly stalking him.

Lucas couldn't relax until he finally made it to the Ministry of Justice. He found his way to the bureaucratic wing to plead his case one more time.

Emanuel dressed for school. He felt oddly fatigued this morning but that didn't stop him. He went to the kitchen and found that his father had left out a small breakfast of milk and toast. Emanuel ate alone to the sounds of hammering and a foul curse word coming from the workshop. Emanuel smiled. If his father was out working in the shop, then they must have given him a new arm when he had went to see the Ministry yesterday. Since Emanuel was sleeping by the time his father had returned, he wasn't able to see the new prosthetic. *After school*, Emanuel told himself as he cleaned up then headed out the door for school.

Emanuel trotted down the front steps and made his way down the walkway. He was relieved that he hadn't seen any sparrows since the day Valentine had taken care of that one. Remembering the event brought an ill feeling to his gut. As he walked, the feeling spread, up his chest to his throat, the sensation was equal parts gripping and painful. He was suddenly gasping for air and leaning against the fence.

"Fath—" was all Emanuel could get out before he collapsed on the sidewalk.

Lucas was working on a small and delicate gear set on the table in front of him, a pair of magnifying spectacles resting on his nose, and a sterile glove on his hand, when a large owl crashed through the window.

Lucas stopped what he was doing, wrapped the parts up in a cloth to keep everything clean, and removed his spectacles.

"The boy!" Valentine was out of breath. "On the sidewalk, down the street. I can't lift him."

In a heartbeat Lucas was dashing out of the house. This was the moment he had been dreading for nine years. He could hear the beating of Valentine's wings, the owl passed him and landed next to a small pile of clothing a few yards away.

Lucas reached the area, nearly out of breath. He crouched down and touched the small form on the ground.

It was his boy alright, pale and lips tinged in blue.

Lucas checked his pulses and found him still alive. *Not for long,* he though as he bent and lifted the child over his shoulder.

"Will he live?" Valentine asked as he took to the air over Lucas's head.

"I'm not sure. I have to take him to the University. I need you to go back to the house and collect everything on the table, bring it to me. When you get to the University, find Dr. Alva C. Mulloy. She's in the lower level. Hurry."

Valentine flew away and Lucas began to run.

Lucas made it to the University in record time, people gasped as they noticed the limp child over his shoulder.

He ran up the campus steps two at a time and into the building, crashed through the stairwell doors, and made his way to the lower level. The path to Alva's laboratory was a familiar one. Lucas had visited her many times; she was an engineer and a doctor, and she had an extraordinarily steady hand.

He burst into Alva's laboratory.

The tall woman turned from her work and removed a pair of goggles. "Lucas?"

He motioned to the boy. "It's time."

He didn't need to say another word before Alva was on the move. She brought him through two more rooms—the path led to the back of her laboratory where she had prepared a space specifically for this day.

The room was cement and cold, but it smelled sterile and was supplied with all of the medical equipment they would need.

Lucas lowered the boy to the bed while Alva washed her hands.

"You sure you want to continue with this?" she asked as she donned gloves and began inspecting the boy. "The surgery is not approved, the first of its kind. If he dies we go to Blackcairne."

"He'll die if we don't try," Lucas replied as he touched his son's cheek.

Valentine flew through the pre-smashed hole in the window. He landed on the table and took in the sight. The blueprints that he so desperately tried to view days ago were laying out, as well as the project Lucas had been working on. And there were two.

Valentine collected everything he saw and then, laying it all in the center of the drape, he grasped the corners, effectively creating a satchel, and flew off to meet Lucas with precious cargo in his talons.

There was a dull *thud* from outside the room and a *whoo*. Lucas left the surgical room and went to find Valentine. The owl had a sack gripped tight in his talons, which he set on the tabletop.

"The boy?" Valentine asked.

Lucas grabbed the sack. "Follow me."

Man and owl ran to where Alva and Emanuel were.

Lucas spread the contents of the makeshift sack on the counter near the far wall. In the few moments that he had been gone, Alva already had the boy hooked up to the machines.

The doctor left the boy's side to inspect what Valentine had delivered.

In the center of the drape there were two clockwork hearts. They looked much like the makings of a timepiece but they were, in fact, hearts.

"Two?" Alva asked. "How?"

Lucas motioned to his missing arm.

"Well," Alva raised a hand to her lips, "an extra will be good. Did you follow my specifications?"

"Precisely," Lucas responded.

"We'll have to autoclave them." Alva picked up one of the small hearts, which was no bigger than her fist. "Did you secure the Black Amber?" she asked as she pressed a finger to the flexible tube where she planned to connect the boy's vena cava.

Lucas was silent.

"How do you expect them to work without the Black Amber?" Alva asked.

"Is there any other way?"

"No." Alva set the heart down. "There is no other way to power the clockwork heart. Without the Black Amber we can't do this."

Lucas glanced at his boy. "How much time do I have?"

"I can't tell you that. When his organic heart gives out, your time is up." Her brow furrowed as she inspected the boy on the bed.

Lucas grabbed one of the hearts off of the table, shoved it in his chest pocket, and ran out of the room.

Lucas entered the Ministry of Justice, Valentine at his side for the first time. In his haste, Lucas forgot his pride and agreed to let Valentine to accompany him.

Lucas headed for the bureaucratic wing, Valentine flying overhead. As he neared the Minister's door, the sea of people parted for them. All except for one woman.

Countess Editha Leah Dellaghy was standing precisely where Lucas needed to go. He had spent nine years avoiding this woman, for good cause. She was Estella's mother and blamed Lucas for the death of her daughter.

"How dare you," the Countess began, "step foot in this building while I am here? We had an agreement."

Her Alderhaben scarf could pay for a barrel of Black Amber on the black market. Lucas had half a mind to rip the garment off of his mother-in-law and use it for just that.

"I did not agree," Lucas replied.

Valentine landed on his shoulder.

The Countess was nearly a replica of his beloved Estella; she had aged well, if not for the animosity in her heart.

"The rumors are true. You come here every week begging. If it's more money you want, forget it!"

"I do not beg for money! I beg to save your grandchild's life." Lucas took an imposing step towards his estranged mother-in-law.

"He should have never been born. That child ended her. And that owl!" The Countess poked a finger at Valentine. "Killed one of my sparrows!"

As far as Lucas was concerned, Valentine did his own bidding; he had no idea what the woman was talking about when it came to the death of a sparrow. He did know that the woman had never met Emanuel; she should have at least put forth some effort before damning the child.

Lucas closed his eyes, clenched his fist. "Perhaps if you had warned Estella of her heart condition we could have been more prepared." Lucas knew he was no better since he'd yet to inform his own son of the hereditary heart condition that was currently draining his life.

"We were trying to protect her. And you… you ruined every plan we ever had for her. And now look at you." She slapped at the hollow sleeve of his missing arm. "You are nothing but—"

"She sounds like a sparrow," Valentine muttered from Lucas's shoulder.

Lucas didn't have the patience for this. Desperate times, desperate measures, and all that; Lucas shoved the woman aside to plead with the man in charge.

Lucas burst through the door of Alva's laboratory, a large vial of Black Amber secured in his hand, Valentine soaring close behind him.

He ran to the surgical room in the back. Emanuel was still breathing, although he was paler and his lips seemed a deeper blue. The boy was draped for surgery, the center of his chest drying with disinfectant.

"Did you get it?" Alva asked from the sink where she was scrubbing her arms up to her elbows.

Lucas held up the vial.

"Brilliant!" Alva's face lit up and for the first time Lucas was struck by how beautiful she was.

Alva crossed the room as she dried her hands. "Open the door of the autoclave, please," she asked Lucas before donning sterile gloves.

He opened the door. Alva waited for the steam to rise before she reached in and pulled out the other clockwork heart. She unscrewed the stopper where the fuel source was to go, this would power the mechanism of the heart and keep it pumping for years to come.

"Pour some in," Alva urged Lucas.

He twisted open the cap on the Black Amber and poured a small amount of the dark liquid into the cask.

Alva secured the stopper and held the heart in her open palm.

"It's not doing anything." Lucas frowned.

"Give it time," Alva whispered.

They waited.

And waited.

And waited.

A sick feeling started to invade Lucas's gut.

Whoo. Valentine muttered.

"Oh, I almost forgot." Alva rotated the heart in her hand.

There was a tinny tick and suddenly the clockwork heart came to life. *Whoosh tick. Whoosh tick.* The little heart chimed as it pumped nothing but air at the moment.

The tick of the heart was a pleasant-sounding delight.

"Oh," Alva smiled wide, "magnificent!" She rushed to the boy and set the clockwork heart amongst her surgical instruments.

Lucas and Valentine watched as the brilliant doctor worked magic.

Lucas woke only to be greeted by the solid cement walls and the cold iron bars of Blackcairne prison. This morning was no different than the past 462 mornings had been. The melancholy in his chest was still there, about the same as it had been over time, definitely less sore than that very first morning after he'd arrived.

Valentine was already awake and perched on the window of their shared cell. "How do you think Alva fared?" The owl refused to look at Lucas.

"She knew the risk, served her time." Lucas groaned as he sat up and settled his bare feet on the cold floor. "Probably still detests me, though."

"Did you ever tell her the entire story of how you procured the Black Amber? The events of that day at the Ministry?"

"Of course not." Lucas shook his head, would never forget what they had done. He was left no choice. It was well worth the risk. "It was better that she didn't know. It was better for her. Shortened her sentence."

"I see."

The remainder of the morning was filled with silence as bird and man contemplated deeply about the event of their lives.

The sound of a baton rapping against the bars of the cell caused Lucas and Valentine to turn their heads.

It was the Minister of Justice.

Lucas stood at attention.

Valentine narrowed his yellow eyes.

The bars slid open and the Minister stepped in.

"Gentlemen," he began as he glanced around the sparse cell, "I see you're both serving your sentences peacefully."

Lucas said nothing.

The Minister sighed deeply as though he was thoroughly bored. "Let's get this over and done with." He reached in his chest pocket, produced a small timepiece, glanced at it then replaced it in his pocket once again. "I'm offering you both an early release. Even after your actions in my office that day."

Lucas was still, waiting for the details before deciding his reaction to the man.

"It's a bit of a compromise. An arrangement, if you will." The Minister tipped his head, waiting for Lucas or Valentine to speak. Neither did. "In exchange for your freedom—a newly initiated good behavior program, really, minted specifically for the two of you—you will commence the rank of Commander Lucas McKenzie. It will be a bit different from your previous rank of Captain, but with a man of your experience, you'll qualify well."

Lucas shifted on his feet. It was a good offer. A real felon would jump on it in a heartbeat.

The Minister raised his brows, as the silence was never-ending in the small cell. "What say you, McKenzie? I've got a newly built proto-submarine with your name on it."

Lucas glanced at Valentine. They were both aware of what they had done, the laws that they broke. This was a chance, but for the old owl to be locked up in a submarine, Lucas worried about his aging friend.

"Oh, come on," the Minister urged. "This is an excellent deal. The best, actually."

Lucas scratched his head, worrying about having been out of the industry for the past ten years. It must not have mattered much if the Minister was here now.

The Minister waved his hand. "It will be just like the old days! Just a bit more water over your head at times." The Minister pressed his lips together.

Lucas opened his mouth to speak.

The Minister raised a finger, stopping him. "There's just one thing. You can't see the boy."

Lucas froze. His heart thumped steady in his chest. "My boy…"

"Precisely. Not even a wink."

"At least tell me how he is?"

"Well. Excellent actually. The Countess has taken quite a liking to him. Dr. Mulloy and yourself saved the boy's life. Too bad such a surgery will never happen again. We can't go replacing organs powered by Black Amber." The Minister tipped his head. "Not unless it's sanctioned by the Ministry, of course."

Lucas exhaled in relief. At least his son was alive and well. The worst of his time in Blackcairne was not knowing the outcome of replacing the sickly heart with the clockwork one. He and Valentine were apprehended before the boy had awoken from surgery.

Lucas didn't know what to say.

The Minister walked out of the room. There was a whisper of voices before he entered again, carrying a package in his hand. The Minister tossed it down on the sparse bed and ripped the paper, revealing what was inside.

"What say you, Captain? We'll even throw in this newfangled prosthetic. Top of the line."

The arm was like nothing Lucas had ever seen. It was brass and leather, so many gears and rods that he couldn't even begin to comprehend how they functioned together.

Even with the arm, Lucas would never be completely whole again. For what they had done, life was a fair sentence. Even though they wouldn't be in Blackcairne, never seeing his child again was punishment enough. At least he knew the boy was well.

Lucas glanced at Valentine.

The owl nodded in agreement.

"We'll take the deal," Lucas said as he reached for the arm.

Nightmare

The earth was crumbling into an abyss, and as Clark stood on the precipice the ground beneath his feet rumbled in defeat. The black hole beckoned as particles of soil and debris spiraled before simply disappearing into space. It was going to devour everything in its path, including Clark.

"We are just going to have to stand here and watch until we die," the old man standing next to Clark shouted. He focused on the void before stepping closer to the crumbling ledge. Whip thin and nearly as naked as Clark; the old man had a thick matting of white hair covering his body, a mild shield from the debris.

"Are you ready?" The old man's beard drifted toward the suction of the abyss.

Clark's gut twisted. "Tell me what you want me to say," he begged. "I don't know what you want. I don't know why I'm here." He was unable to move his body more than a few millimeters in any direction. He was frozen.

"Don't you remember?" the old man asked.

Clark shook his head. The last memory he had was spending a quiet evening at home. He'd read his seven-year-old son a book before tucking him into bed, he'd watched the final minutes of the Syracuse basketball game on the television, then he'd showered and crawled into bed next to his wife. He'd kissed her goodnight before settling next to her, wishing she'd worn something else to bed besides his old stained T-shirt and a pair of baggy sweatpants. Clark glanced down and noticed he was wearing the same plaid boxer shorts. Simple dissatisfaction was the worst of his sins tonight, it certainly didn't warrant this.

"I want a revelation." The old man's beard drifted in the sucking wind and bristled against Clark's arm.

The earth crumbled. Rocks and chunks of soil fell and disappeared into the point of no return. The land beneath his feet roared as another twelve inches crumbled. It was getting closer. This land was giving up.

Clark shivered as the old man's coarse hair drifted up his arm; goose bumps raised his skin as the hair glided over his shoulder and to the side of his face. He tried to tilt his head away but he was but he wasn't able to move far. The long whiskers tickled his lips before finding their way inside his mouth and sticking to the dry mucous membranes. Clark spat and pushed at the whiskers with his tongue before the old man took notice and smoothed his hand over the length of beard and twisted it neat.

"You want a revelation?" Clark asked. "A revelation of what?"

Tumbleweed blew past. Followed by another and another. The hot wind was relentless as clusters of dried, heat-crusted stems barraged Clark's backside. They scraped at his bare legs and back, tearing his skin. Warm blood dripped down his calf only to be sucked away with the wind.

"Revelations to offer as penance as we watch the flatness of earth crumble away." The man gripped a knotted cane that was jabbed securely in the dry soil beneath their bare feet. "It will help pass the time. At least."

Clark blinked in disbelief. "The earth is not flat."

The soil was quick to release the cane the old man was leaning on; he whipped it and struck Clark on the sensitive bone of his shin.

"What the fuck?" Clark yelled. "What was that for?"

"This earth is flat." The old man corrected him. "Right here, right now, it is as flat as it will ever be." He twisted his gray beard into submission again. "It's just a hot, flat earth underneath all of the bullshit. It was never round. The roundness was a mirage bending under the façade of science."

Clark opened to dispute the thought of a flat earth again, but the old man struck him again with the cane before he could speak. He'd hit the shin, this time breaking the skin. Specks of blood from the wound were drawn away with the white-hot tumbleweeds, everything smoldered as they swirled in the distance.

It had only been a few minutes, Clark guessed, between the groans near the edge of the land. More dirt and rocks crumbled and were sucked away, only to circle the drain in the event horizon that was forever moving closer. Clark knew that soon it would be more than his blood in that swirling pool. Soon it would be his whole body. And then what would become of him?

"God damn it," Clark muttered as he sucked in a breath.

"Don't curse in this place," the old man warned. "You don't want them to hear you."

"Them?" Clark asked, his voice reaching a pitch. He tried to turn his head but was unable.

"The young ones." The old man ticked his head to the space behind them. "Memories from long ago."

As far as Clark knew it was only the two of them standing alone in this place. It was the worst nightmare Clark had ever experienced. He squeezed his eyes closed and tried to wake up. He tried to remember the feel of the pillow top mattress underneath him; he tried to remember the feel of his soft wife cuddling close under the blankets. He tried to remember the feel of her small hand as she stroked him.

"The young ones will come back to haunt you," the old man continued. "Things that go bump in the night, things you think you forgot, things you tucked away to never see the light of day again."

The white hair on the man's chest wavered in the wind. He jabbed the cane into the ground again to steady himself, the sinew muscles of his thin arms bulging.

Clark didn't have any childhood fears. Not like his own boy who feared the dark, the kid refused to walk to his room alone past sunset. Clark feared nothing though. He'd spent half of his life jumping out of planes and surfing shark-infested seas and running toward fires, running toward danger.

"You think you are brave," the man warned. "But you need to listen."

Thud-thudthud-thud-thudthud. The sound of something approaching fast and strong rang out behind them. It was an uneven galloping of an object that was both dense and enormous; the ground trembled underneath their feet but this time it was not due to the crumbling terrain. This sound brought fear. It was as though a freight train were traveling a thousand miles per hour and headed straight for them.

"Release me!" Clark shouted. "It's going to hit us." He couldn't turn to see what it was but his spine tingled with knowing fear. Whatever it was barreling at them would kill him on impact. "Now!"

His muscles around his spine tightened further with dread.

"No." The man settled his palms on the grip of the cane. "We wait for this."

Clark tried to bend his knees and drop his body to the ground for safety but his knees would only bend the tiniest bit. He tried to wiggle his feet but he was only able to disturb a small bit of soil around his heels. Whatever force was holding him in place would not budge.

The roaring sound of a thousand mustangs galloping unevenly moved closer. Dirt and rocks pelted his back as they were sucked into the abyss with welcome. The black hole before them was never sated; it was going to take everything.

"Break me free!" Clark begged the old man as a pebble struck the back of his thigh, embedding itself in muscle. The tissue of his body did not stop the rock, the abyss sucked it forward. Clark screamed as the pebble tore through muscle and tendon, he screamed louder as it scraped and broke the compact bone of his femur before invading the marrow. With a sick popping sound, the rock evacuated through the front of his thigh and glided at lightning speed into the blackness.

"Holy fuck," Clark cried. "What the fuck is wrong with you?" he swore at the old man. "Let me—"

The old man struck him in the stomach with the cane. "Here it comes," he warned. "Steady yourself."

The beast behind them was a second away. It groaned as a train in a tornado, it's bulk slammed into the earth and shook the ground before rolling and charging closer and closer and closer.

Every hair on Clark's body stood on end. He had nowhere to hide.

"It's here." The old man fanned his fingers calmly over the cane's grip.

It struck the ground. *Thud*. It bounced, airborne as it rolled, *sssswack-wack-wack*.

It whipped Clark's back from shoulder to buttock a dozen times before it slammed close to his heels. Clark was sure he was about to fall into a cavern created by the giant mass behind him. But while the ground flexed and his gut dropped in near-vomit inducing dread, the thing went airborne. Something jabbed into his back on both sides of his shoulder blades. It stabbed into the bone and tugged. Clark roared in pain, knowing he would most likely be torn in two by the forces holding his body still and the thing rolling in flight above his head. The pain was unbearable as he felt the muscles of his abdomen separate and his intestines stretch. Then, something snapped. The pressure on his shoulders released as the rolling freight train passed overhead.

Clark glanced up. It wasn't a train or a beast. It was a giant weeping willow tree. Its long sweeping branches whipped about the trunk as the tree rolled through the air brutally. The willow leapt into the abyss as easy as a penny tossed into a fountain. Its massive trunk groaned, the bark shattering under the force of the black hole and the force of the tree's own inner core.

Clark had never seen anything so graceful and violent.

He'd survived.

He'd survived!

Clark exhaled in relief. He'd outlasted the giant willow tree with a simple hole in his leg and the pain in his shoulders. Clark flexed his arms and twisted his torso doing his best to figure out what injuries he'd sustained.

"Release me." Clark said as blood oozed down his back.

The old man shrugged. "A tiny bit, perhaps." He tapped his cane on the ground twice.

The magic that held him steady eased. Clark could finally move his head freely. He looked down to see the ragged ends of two tree branches jutting out the front of his shoulders. The pungent scent of the broken green inner core of a young branch scored his nostrils. "Oh god!" Clark started to breathe heavy. "Oh god, oh god, oh god." The jagged edges of the tree branches curled around the curve of his clavicles. The end of the branch continued to coil, over his back and under his armpits, and then twining together across his chest. He looked behind him, tilted his shoulder as far forward as he could only to find two long branches of the willow tree jutting from his back with the long elliptical curve of mayfly wings.

"No!" Clark shouted at the strange sight. "No! No! No!"

The edge of the earth thundered as more land fell away.

Clark knew it wouldn't stop. He squeezed his eyes closed. *Wake up, wake up, wake up*, was his internal mantra. He did his best to remember the good times. The day he met Megan at college, the day she said yes after he proposed, those hot nights as they explored each other's bodies, the birth of his son… his mind wandered to darker memories, sinful memories. He shook his head to escape them. He didn't want to revisit what he'd buried in the past.

"The edge will reach us soon." The old man breathed in deep through his nostrils, knowingly.

"Underneath all the bullshit. This earth is as flat as your lies. As flat as that fog you separate your brain with."

Clark turned his head but the man was out of his periphery. *Wake up, wake up, wake up*, he whispered to himself. The longer his eyes were closed the less he felt the suck of the black hole. He could feel the firm pillow underneath his head, Megan's softness curled around him, the sound of the bedroom door opening as their son crawled into their bed. Clark wanted to hold his son one last time, he wanted to rub his hand on the boy's head and teach him how to throw a baseball. He wanted to take the boy horseback riding on the Maryland beaches and driving a hundred miles an hour on the Arizona flats. He didn't want it all to end like this. Early.

Clark opened his eyes at the arid creak of wood rubbing on wood.

More dirt and rock dribbled into the void.

Clark turned his head, searching for his companion.

The old man stepped forward and pressed his lips together in disappointment. "Now, here comes another."

The dry creaking of old wood struggling to maintain its strength grew louder. *Slap slap slap,* went the sound of long boards breaking loose and knocking into each other. This zephyr brought the reek of manure. Clark coughed and gagged.

"The stench didn't seem to bother you before," the old man said.

Dust gathered around them, blocking out most of the dank light.

"I can barely see," Clark said as he blinked, doing his best to keep the sand out of his eyes.

The ground shuddered as the dull sound of dense wood thundering in movement drew closer. The wind tugged at the branches extending from his back, the movement strained his muscles and tore at his flesh. The wind hallowed through the gaping wound in his thigh drawing fresh blood.

The sound of a horse baying broke through the racket, then a cow moaning, followed by the stuttered gloat of a goat. Clark twisted his head. A giant barn was rolling toward them, roof over gaping-bottom it rolled and rolled and rolled with loud thumps. The slats of wood wavered as a wind chime in a storm. It was lumbering closer, the farm animals rolling inside like dice shaken in a cup.

Fear slid up Clark's spine as he envisioned the flat side of the barn spreading his guts in the dirt beneath his feet. Clark did his best to ignore the pain in his thigh and shoulders and struggled to get loose. But only his head would move. His body was still as a statue.

"We must endure this," the old man said.

There was a sickening splat of a fluid filled carcass hitting the ground to the left. Clark whipped his head to the side to see the body of the goat had fallen free of the rolling barn only to be slammed into the ground, it's neck broken with a sad short bleat. It was the last sound that goat would ever make before it was carried away into the churning void, looking nothing more than a farm toy in a bathtub circling the drain.

Clark had recognized the goat as it flew past him; he recognized the brown dots and the chest of white. It was his mother's goat that lived for many years on their farm as nothing more than a pet. A memory flashed, that teenage angst which overcame him one too many times. Clark shook his head and tried his best to forget the memory that he'd buried deep, but it was hard to forget the sticky warmth of the goat, the memory of his first orgasms, the dank smell of that barn in the middle of the night.

"What else have you probed your slippery dick with?" the old man asked.

"Fuck you!" Clark screamed at the man. "Go fuck yourself."

"Don't curse in this place." The old man clucked his tongue. "You don't want them to hear you."

Thud thud thud. The barn rolled closer. Slivers of wood whipped past them, slicing tiny cuts into Clark's arms. He tipped his head, chin to chest, and shrugged his shoulders, trying his best to protect himself from the barn. The long side of the barn slammed into the ground before them. It rolled, tilted up on the peak of the upside down roof and wavered as though it knew Clark was there. Waiting.

"Here it comes," the old man warned.

Darkness fell over them as the barn tipped. The suction of the air underneath the structure was strong, it took the breath from his lungs. Shit fell from the breaks in the boards and pelted him in the head before it too was drawn away to the abyss. The barn, however, was too large to be sucked away so easily. It tilted and groaned as it fell to its side.

"Rel-aaaagh!" Clark was about to scream, "Release me!" as the window opening fell directly over him, saving him from being splattered by the broad side of the barn. Glass shattered over his head, and in the split second that his tongue was enunciating the long l-sound of release; a shard of glass split his tongue in two.

Blood pooled in Clark's mouth as the barn groaned. Still rolling with inertia it tipped away, revealing he'd barely been touched, save for his forked tongue. The barn angled toward space and teetered on the edge of the crumbling earth before falling into the abyss. It circled twice before the forces of the black hole tore it apart, breaking it into a billion matchsticks.

The animals were stunned with fear, their legs stiff and bodies trembling with bloat. The force of the hole stretched their skin; it twisted the connective tissue and broke the threads of collagen that held the creatures together. They exploded from the middle first with secretions and organs flying in all directions before swirling along with the rest of the debris.

"My *th*ounge!" Clark stuck his tongue out to see the damage that had been done. The large muscle burned as blood trickled down the sides of his mouth. "Ugh. *Th*ucking relea*th* me!" he begged.

The old man patted him on the arm. "You do have the devil's tongue."

Clark closed his mouth; his throat swelling and stomach churning as blood dripped down his esophagus. He coughed and retched. He turned his head to the side and spit. If he ever made it out of this place, he doubted Megan would ever take him back now that he'd been maimed so badly. Even after all of their years together, even after he'd stuck by her side as she swelled with child and never lost the weight. He'd only stepped out on her a time or two or four, just enough to relieve his angst since she wouldn't touch him in the ninth month. Clark hadn't felt any guilt about it. Especially after the birth of the boy who'd left her with a fourth-degree perineal tear. He'd stuck by her side as she sat on ice packs and he'd bought her a lifetime supply of stool softeners. He stopped begging her for sex and waited until she was ready. She might never be ready again if she saw him like this. Now that he had a hole in his leg and tree branches in his shoulders and a torn tongue. He wondered if she'd ever look at him again.

A feeling of warmth in Clark's mouth interrupted his thoughts. The bleeding had slowed and it seemed it was already healing. Maybe his tongue would heal on it's own? Maybe she'd take him back, mutilated as he was.

"I give up," Clark said.

"You never give up. You endure." The old man raised his fist, the thick white hair on his arm wavering in the breeze. "You sustain with bravery." He lifted the cane with his other hand and poked it in the direction of the void. "We are facing the edge of the earth together! Physicist and Astrologists have dreamt of this moment."

"No, they haven't. The earth is not flat."

The wiry old man twirled, kicking up dust just before he stomped a foot on the ground in a defensive stance, facing Clark. He swung his cane and hit Clark in the injured thigh.

"Go*th*amn it!" Clark groaned.

The earth thundered and nearly four feet of dirt crumbled off the ledge near them.

"We ha*the* to get out of here." Clark warned. "We ha*the* to go before we fall in." He tried to move his legs but the tensing of his muscled only brought sharp pain to the wound in his leg. "Relea*the* me!"

"Wait, there's more. Oh this one," the old man said. "You might like this one. This one brings truth you've suppressed for ages."

There were moans and the slick slapping of skin on skin, touching, massaging, and sliding together in sweaty ecstasy. Then came the wet suction of a woman in heat, calling out in ecstasy as though she were being probed over and over again. Clark felt the organ between his legs swell. He couldn't help it. He turned his head to the side, twisting as far as he could to get a glance. This had always been his weakness.

Naked bodies rolled and tumbled toward them. Articles of clothing flew out of the middle of the tangle of arms and legs. Breasts jiggled, a dick jutted out, a dainty pointed foot with red painted toenails extended in his direction. Women and men alike groaned in bliss as they rolled along shameless in their nakedness.

A shirt billowed around Clark's head flying away like a feather in the wind. Next came a bra, two socks, panties, a pair of jeans, then a pair of short shorts. The tangle of bodies called his name, "Clark. Clark-boy. Clarky." They whispered the wicked things they'd do to his body. "Come with us." The tangle came closer and closer and closer. He could smell the sweat and the semen and the blood. It was the blood that made him exhale with want. He couldn't deny it. The bodies tumbled, but they never came close enough for him. The gyrating and pounding figures rolled off the edge of the flat earth without giving him the sweet release they'd promised.

Clark exhaled in disappointment. He'd managed to forget the pain for a few minutes, but now it returned with rage, the worst of it at his back. He turned and saw that something had become tangled in the willow branches. Something he wanted to see. Something to add to the dark fantasy. Something he'd tried to bury.

Clark wiggled his shoulders and did his best to disturb the branches. The object finally released and Clark got a good look at it before it trailed away. It was a small white sneaker well worn and stained with dirt. That was a child's shoe. The sneaker of a little girl. A dark memory twisted his gut, a sinful memory, one he should never be satisfied with remembering, but the swelling between his legs remained.

Clark's mouth went dry, his stomach contracted with the fear of being caught, sweat beaded his brow. Someone had seen him.

"Beg for a witness." The old man tapped his cane.

"A witness for what?" Clark was distracted.

"You want them to see you. You want them to see *this*." The old man jutted his cane toward the flaming shoe circling the abyss. "You want them to see us. It's the only way. Without a witness you will never be saved."

Burning sweat was dripping into Clark's eyes. "Witness me!" Clark screamed into what was left of the edge of the earth.

The edge crumbled as five more feet sunk away. The edge was too close now. Clark could spit into it now.

Thunder cracked but it sounded strange, like a long foghorn. Clark looked up but there were no clouds in the sky. There were only twinkling stars, judging him and the old man.

Brrroooom. Came the sound from behind them.

The old man nodded. "Ah. Another."

It was the sound of a large boulder being dragged across the dry earth.

Clark turned.

The hot wind blew.

The dark hole beckoned.

Brroooom. Brrooom. It creaked until the object finally came into view. It was an old farmhouse sliding across the burnt soil. It left a solid track and berms of dirt in its wake as it was tugged across the land. It moved closer and closer. Clark was sure it was going to slide over him and push him over the edge before the earth could fall away on it's own. The house didn't push him over, instead it slid close, the corner of the porch rubbed against his arm, pushing him out of the way. Clark couldn't move and the edges of the porch rubbed harder, pushing slivers into his skin as it passed. The basement bricks rubbed against his right foot, tearing the skin away, revealing flesh and bone.

Clark screamed in pain as the house dragged pieces of his flesh with it. After a few moments, when the pain was no longer new and he could get a grip, Clark examined the sides of the house and recognized farmhouse he grew up in. The house tipped off the edge of the earth and fell into the void.

The whitewash planks of the exterior chipped in the force of the burning wind. The front door slammed open and closed in rapid sharp thuds before it was ripped from its hinges and flew apart off the house. The planks of the porch twisted and broke apart into fine slivers. The roof tiles slid off like a fish skinned of its scales. The house twisted from cube to prism to cylinder as dimensions shifted. The windows shattered, the glass melting in the heat of the vortex. It was no longer the simple white house of his childhood; it was a dark twisted place of sin.

"Do you see it?" the old man asked. "Right there! There you are." He pointed. "Witness your debaucheries."

Clark squinted, focusing on the upper bedroom of the house. He saw himself as a teenager. The sheets of his bed tacked to the wall creating a dark fort underneath. He couldn't turn away from the arrogant satisfied look on the face of his teenage self. There was someone else under those sheets, someone small whom he could control. Someone whose mother was too tired to care. Someone who wouldn't say a thing about what he was doing.

The house burst into a million pieces.

Clark knew he was in deep shit.

"Get me the *th*uck out of here!" Clark screamed at the old man. "Megan!" Clark shouted. "Megan, wake me up! Wake up! Wake up! Wake *me* up!" Clark closed his eyes and shook his head vigorously from side to side. Of course the fat cow wouldn't wake up to save him. He'd spend weeks squatting next to the toilet to help spray her damaged lady parts clean after the baby just like the nurses in the hospital showed him. She never did anything like that for him. He could almost hear her snoring next to him, the rattle in her throat breaking the sound barrier and voiding him of sleep.

The earth shuddered in disgust before another large chunk broke off. The edge was a mere twenty centimeters from the tip of his toes. The dirt underneath his bloody and bare feet shifted but Clark stood steady, rooted the ground as he'd been since he opened his eyes.

"I warned you not to curse on this earth." The old man jabbed Clark in the foot with the cane. "I told you it would bring the young ones."

"You're so full of shit," Clark yelled. "Release me!"

The energy of the air behind them shifted. This wasn't a house, or a barn, or a whipping willow tree. No. There was a *thing* directly behind Clark. Maybe it was a few hundred feet maybe a few meters. It was small and dark and Clark could feel its presence with every molecule of his body. It changed shape, wavering between solid and fluid as it moved closer. It was familiar.

"It's here," the old man warned calmly.

"What's here? What is it?" Clark though of the memories of the house and the barn. Had he done worse?

The thing slinked closer.

One moment it was solid and apprehensive, the next it was liquid and curious. It was close.

Clark looked down as an inky liquid pooled around his feet. It moved closer, shimmering and vibrating. It stopped near the side of his foot, inspecting inquisitively before sliding over his toes and examining the portion of his right foot that the farmhouse had rubbed off.

It wrapped around his ankle. The dark substance slithered up his calf; it swathed and glided leaving a damp trail of mucus in its wake. It didn't stop. It crept, exploring the dark hair that coated his leg. Clark shook his limb, trying to scare the thing away but it did nothing. It slithered into the gaping wound of his thigh, stretching the edges of skin uncomfortably as Clark groaned, his stomach queasy from the sensation. It continued moving, up into the leg of his boxers, over the concave bone of his hip, across the small of his back, it circled his buttocks and rolled between the crevice before slithering over his anus, which puckered and retracted in fear. It didn't stop. It slithered in to explore and Clark recognized the wet probing and lapping of a wicked tongue.

"*Th*op," Clark begged. The knowing fear of inevitable penetration was strong. "Please *th*op."

It stopped and slid away in an instant. Much more responsive than when the same request had been begged of him in his teenage bedroom. The black ink pooled at his feet again before moving away and changing form. The substance grew taller, forming legs, a torso, arms, and a head. The black shifted to skin and clothing and hair. It changed into a girl.

Clark recognized her. He recognized her pale skin, perfect and soft, he knew because he'd stroked that skin before. Her blonde hair was pulled into pigtails. She wore only one white Nike shoe well worn and stained with dirt. It was Gwen.

Gwen was a dark secret he'd planned to take to his grave. She'd been so perfect, there was more than one night since then that he'd thought of her. There was more than one night he'd closed his eyes as he pounded away at Megan and envisioned Gwen in her place. Oh, he'd done bad and he'd imagined worse.

He'd ruined Gwen. Clark could see it in the way she stared at him. Eyes devoid of life, skin devoid of blood, she was a shell devoid of life.

"Don't tell your mom," Gwen's haunted voice whispered. She pointed at him, her arm transforming into the fluid black substance and shooting into his mouth. It spread his lips, stretching him uncomfortably. The blunt tip probed the back of his throat, gagging him. "Look what you made me do." Her voice cracked, turning from that of a sweet girl to a gnarled witch. "This is just between us. Forever." She jabbed her liquid arm harder into the back of his throat. "Do you remember? I never forgot. And it ended me."

Tears stung Clark's eyes as he heaved. He knew he deserved this. He deserved this more than Gwen deserved to be found hanging in that barn one year after that night.

"You made me do it!" She jabbed him one last time before retracting her arm.

Clark twisted his head to the side and vomited.

Gwen disappeared in a wisp of white smoke. She left behind the scent of freshly cut pasture grass, the pungent aroma of dandelions on the farmhouse table, the fragrance of childhood memories he'd ruined for her. And more she'd never live to experience. The smoke didn't dissipate; instead it rolled toward him, barreling down his open mouth.

The flat earth shuddered in disgust.

The old man whispered, "Witness me."

The ground gave away under Clark's feet. He fell, cycling his arms trying to grasp at something, anything, the edge of the crumbling earth or a root or a large jutting rock or the helpful extended hand of the old man. But there was nothing. He wished, as strange as it sounded that he could flap the willow branch wings and fly. He couldn't and he didn't. Clark screamed in panic as he drifted away from the edge of earth in a slow descent to nothingness, clawing and grasping the air with dirt-stained hands.

The old man stepped forward. "Witness me!" he shouted into the void. "Witness me! I have done as you've asked."

Lightning cracked and Clark recognized the old man in the flash of light. It was himself, old and withered.

Clark's eyes flashed open. His hands spread across the pillowtop mattress beneath him. The soft body of Megan rubbed against his side. He jerked into a sitting position. It was a dream, a horrible horrible nightmare. Nothing more. He rubbed his face, feeling the grit of dirt left behind. "What is this?"

"What's wrong?" Meg leaned away to switch the nightstand light on.

Pain gripped Clark's chest and tore down his left arm. His tongue was thick in his mouth and dizziness overtook his consciousness.

"*Th*-omething-*th* wrong." Clark began to panic as he recognized his slurred speech. He felt hot and cold simultaneously. His arm was numb and his heart quivered in his chest.

"What's wrong with you?" Megan's eyes were wide with concern as she reached forward and touched his nose. Black ooze coated her fingertip and she inspected it, sniffing the substance. "It smells like... grass." Megan's face twisted in confusion.

Clark dropped backward on the bed.

"I'm going to call 9-1-1." Megan rolled away and ran out the bedroom door.

In the moment that passed Clark hated her for making him agree to the no electronics in the bedroom rule.

He felt the back of his throat swell, ready to expel the beer he'd drank earlier while watching the game. He heaved and black ink spilled from his mouth. It didn't pool on the sheets as it should have, the blackness moved with the viscosity of honey. Dribbling down his cheek and collecting itself in a ball before extending to the ceiling and transforming into a figure.

Gwen was there.

"This earth is not flat," Clark said. "You don't belong here."

Gwen hovered above him. "There was a time that I belonged here and not on the plane of your sins."

There were shouts from downstairs, the echoes of men pounding on the front door of his house. Megan's voice was frantic as she did her best to describe what was happening to Clark.

Gwen's specter flitted to the bedroom door and slammed it closed before hovering over him again.

Heavy footfalls ran up the stairs. The door handle twisted.

Black liquid shot from Gwen's arms and penetrated Clark's shoulders, another tore through his leg leaving a gaping hole in its wake. Another probed his mouth and tore his tongue into a serpent's bifurcation.

Gwen's form dissipated to fog and fell slowly over Clark's still body, absorbing everything that she was until there was nothing, just as he'd done all those years ago.

The door crashed open. The E.M.Ts stopped in their tracks as they took in the scene of the cooling corpse on the bed.

Megan pushed her way closer, stopping to scream in disgust when she saw what her husband had transformed into. His torn tongue poked from the corner of his mouth, large black holes bore through his shoulders, another through his leg, and the black liquid had trailed along the mattress leaving the impression of the mayfly wings Clark had been gifted with on the plane of his depravities.

One of the E.M.T's pulled a cell phone from his pocket and snapped a picture. "No one is going to believe this," he muttered.

CONSEQUENCE OF GRAVITY.
POETRY.

Diary of a Space Cadaver

There is nothing but carrion

and broken toys

floating fast enough to impale.

I want to believe

in more than plastics.

More than the emissions of burning rocket fuel.

I can no longer stand the sweet smell of prairie grass

the tang of fresh cut dandelion

the fresh murk of ponds and valley streams

the chirp of crickets the slow buzz of fat bumble bees

the hallow knock of a wind chime.

Those memories make me ill.

I've made conclusions

after all.

Died in installments over a million years.

Broke my back over snowcapped mountains

drowned in lush green forests

bathed in waterfalls.

We had a truce of six million years.

And I strung

dainty stars of the finest silver across the Milky Way

in celebration.

I painted dust plumes of lilac and Galaxy blue.

I gave everything.

I wonder if maybe there is a space roach in my ear

whispering devious things?

Turned to tar from a hundred years of decomposition.

it speaks to me

after all this time.

My scaled back aches.

Pockmarks from eons of debris mar my ribcage.

My wings spread, a blanket of darkness.

I want to

smother the flames of this wrath.

Bodies float by.

Frozen.

Bloated.

A memory of what they once were.

Who they once were.

Unlike me.

I'm still here.

Alive.

Always.

Diaspora

I watched my homeland crumble.

Wells went dry,

tanks ran empty.

Family went scarce

in time of need.

Rows of paint-chipped houses were all that was left.

Surrounded by a cerulean smog,

the hard days were winning.

This new madness was everywhere.

I went to the stars for answers.

I transcended through time.

Thousands of light years away,

there was an answer blinking back at me.

There was more out there than yesterday.

More than this muddy bleakness.

There's courage in leaving.

Hope in

rebirth.

You can't run away,

They told me.

Still.

I went.

Closer to the stars and the moon.

To be surrounded by salt and humidity

oceans not crimson rivers.

Forests draped in vines and a drawl greeted me.

Go, the stars told me,

where the moon pulls the tide.

The land is dry, sand and crisp grass bite.

Wolves and coyotes howl names into the vastness of

night.

I went.

I learned to slink out of the heat,

became serpentine, a creature of twilight and daybreak.

I found stillness.

I learned to

pause.

I learned to suspend in time like Spanish moss on a

majestic oak.

This is

the way I live now.

Blood thinned and skin burnt,

pieces of my homeland, melted off me
in layers of ochre.
Those who came with didn't recognize me
after the transformation.

I know one thing now.
This is where the world ends.
In heat
and haste.

Mission to Mars

I am a rocket woman
gravity and time are lost to me
I am all dials and tethers when I wake
Clicking carabineers to keep me grounded in place
instead of the pitter-patter of my children's feet
Click. Click. Click.

This artificial light surrounds me
instead of the golden sun
blue and woke
My pupils fixate on monitors
I work without time, without interruption
My melatonin is wonked
My last peaceful sleep
unknown
Get some sunshine, they suggest
But, clicking on the natural-light mood-bed
is too hard right now
Click. Click. Click.

Two-hundred Sols
That Red Planet is closer than ever before
Don't rush, they said
I've retained fuel
slowed only to increase my radiation exposure
So many are depending on you
they said
Fingers hovering over the keyboard
My heart filled with guilt at every decision
Preserve as much as you can, they said
My cheeks are hallowed
Click. Click. Click.

I dream of blastoff
Thrusters fuel burning clouds of smoke
Astronauts of old have said people used to line the beach
to watch
There were none for me
No sandy Cocoa Beach, no lulling Atlantic waves
It was a dry desert a torn open aquifer
a waitlist for those lucky enough to man the next mission
or ride along

I am a rocket woman
procedure and schedule are everything to me
The cargo hold is everything Costco used to be
Five tons of pure Russian vodka
Ten tons of powdered milk
Twenty tons of beef
Thirty tons of pulverized dried and vacuum-sealed fruit
Forty tons of unlabeled electronics
Toss half the food in an emergency they said
49.99 tons of pure Russian vodka
I edit the cargo hard copy and take a sip
Click. Click. Click.

Posters still line the walls for Zero G games
Arrows lead to game rooms filled with hydroponics
Strawberry fields listen to Sweet Home Alabama
The module instructions say something softer, classical,
Kenny G or Mozart.
But Fuji apple branches grow stronger with a head-
banging
heavy beat from those drums
There is strength in music

that the vacuum of space cannot steal

After 11 hours sleep, a hot cup of coffee
I sing again.
My voice is foreign and dry
cracks break through when a lyric reminds me of them
I sing again
until a reminder alarm that I've passed the halfway mark
Until the blue light draws my gaze
binders of SOPs call my name.
Dials need recording, volumes need documenting,
an empty restaurant needs eaten in
Click. Click. Click.

I am not the woman they think I am
They shouldn't have told me to bring the pictures
They shouldn't have sent the voice memos and videos
The expanse outside this porthole leaves me feeling
empty
I am told I have much to be thankful for
I was chosen for being strong, smart, stable
Here I am yearning for the

time before we decided to leave earth
Click. Click. Click.

All I ever do is say goodbye
Twenty or so trips they'd told me
Not Monday through Friday
Twenty months between weekends off
filled with laundry and meals eaten in awkward small
talk
Their smiles are empty with the forced homecoming
Worse her smell lingers in the couch pillows
they forgot to hide her shirts in the closet
Sunday I pack my bags, preflight
empty kisses and finger-tip touches tell me goodbye
again.
A man can't wait this long
Click. Click. Click.

I can't go back to that place that felt like home
There is no alternative now
Mars isn't a place to raise children
It's too cold here

cold as a burnt-out fuse
it's drawn my warmth into the dry, rusted dust clouds
I am more alien than human now

I am a rocket woman
duty is everything to me
My starship is empty
Now a vessel without use
After three trips to this Red Planet
there's enough cargo for my rocket ship
to be filled with people on the next round
It's hard to imagine the cargo bay filled with suitcases,
theaters,
restaurants filled with couples.

The return is draining
I've stared too long at plumes of stardust
it sticks to my clothes clouds my eyes.
I am radioactive, an asteroids' afterthought
Indie rock echoes in the empty passages
I scream lyrics in an empty cockpit
My handwriting in the logs is bold, pressed hard

anticipating what is to come.
Click. Click. Click.

Three-quarters of the way home

a weekly voice message bleeps on the screen

It's not good

My camera zooms in on earth, the continents are

pockmarked

more than ever before

It would be pedal-to-the-metal if I were driving

Instead I suffer in cruise-mode

Click. Click. Click.

After six-hundred Sols

my home is gone

a crater on the face of North America

Re-entry is rough

There's the sickness of velocities

gravity that my body has forgotten

Now there is the sorrow of my children not being here

Neither is my husband

They've never missed a landing

even when she asked them to

I am a rocket woman
life is everything to me
This ship is my womb
The line is long, the refuel quick
There isn't time for weekend relief
For the first time my cargo holds humans
not one of them my own
We are joined by an umbilical tether to Mars
Click. Click. Click.

Life on Mars

We reached through time
to get here.
Fold upon fold upon fold
Dimension to dimension
A skip
hop and
a jump.

We deserve this
red dirt,
thin air,
threatening moons lingering in the distance.
A cold heart centers this plane.
Ages of burning jet fuel couldn't warm it.
Nor the butterscotch horizon.

We fell out of the sky
Tore a hole to the left of the moon and jumped.
We couldn't be what we were before.
No gods and monsters.
Just rusted blank slate.

Rocket woman's ship was full,
There were no more flights.
All we had left was time
To Fold upon fold upon fold upon.

A few hundred made it.
Grabbed everything we could carry.
Equipment left in piles in the desert
Were ours for the taking.

Here we wait.
Eyes to the sky
As the last of us touches down.
Eager for oxygen and heat.
Ravenous, really.

There is something
Buried beneath this red dirt.
Something more than ash,
More than desiccated bone.
There are no
heroes down here.

Consequence
of
Gravity

About the Author

M. R. Pritchard is a two-time Kindle Scout winning author and her short story "Glitch" has been featured in the 2017 winter edition of THE FIRST LINE literary journal. She holds degrees in Biochemistry and Nursing. She is a northern New Yorker transplanted to the Gulf Coast of Florida who enjoys coffee, cloudy days, and reading on the lanai.

To receive updates on new releases, sign up for her newsletter at http://eepurl.com/TXnkL

Visit her website MRPritchard.com or her blog http://secretlifeofatownie.blogspot.com/ where she writes about all things books.

A Note from the author:

If you enjoyed Consequence of Gravity, please leave a review, tell a friend, or gift to a friend. These small acts keep authors like me writing. Thank you.